PERFECT BEAUTIES

A DR HARRISON LANE MYSTERY
BOOK 5

GWYN BENNETT

Storm

To request permissions, contact the publisher at rights@stormpublishing.co

Ebook ISBN: 978-1-80508-021-3
Paperback ISBN: 978-1-80508-022-0

Cover design: Tash Webber
Cover images: Alamy (RF), Shutterstock

Published by Storm Publishing.
For further information, visit:
www.stormpublishing.co

ALSO BY GWYN BENNETT

1

He smiled kindly at her. He was always so gentle. So sympathetic.

'Look how beautiful you are,' he said, and turned the mirror around to show her.

She stared at the face looking back at her, and a single tear slipped from her right eye.

'I know. Wonderful, isn't it?' He smiled again, pride filling his chest.

The woman in the mirror said nothing. No smile creased her perfectly sculptured features. Her lips, plumped to perfection, didn't say a word.

She was everything she'd ever wanted to be. As gorgeous as all the best Instagram influencers, the cast of *Love Island*, or the models on the pages of *Vogue*. He was right. The woman in the mirror was beautiful. Even her body was slim and defined, her breasts firm and waist tiny. Her skin soft, smooth, and tight. Blonde hair flowed around her face, silky and shiny. Her eyes, a bright, vivid sapphire blue, were framed by thick, long lashes.

She was unrecognisable. The mirror woman wasn't her.

'I have kept my side of the deal,' he said, putting the mirror down. There was that smile again. When she'd first met him, it had seemed paternal, the father she'd never had.

She knew better now.

'You will be famous beyond your wildest dreams. Your beautiful face will be on every front page of every newspaper in the world. Social media will buzz with nothing else but you.' A sigh of pleasure escaped him.

Once, that had been all she'd ever craved.

Her bright-blue eyes moved from him to the operating table behind, and the electric saw. Inside her perfect body, a scream began to form.

He took her hand, gently leading her. His soft eyes, warm with smile lines at their outer corners, never left her face.

'It's time for your side of our deal. Then, our perfect story will be complete.'

2

Dr Harrison Lane was sitting at a pub table with DS Jack Salter, and the two of them had already downed several pints. The evidence was stacking up in front of him; empty glasses that spoke of a broken resolve. Jack was laughing in his face, telling him he wasn't a man if he didn't have another drink. His throat burned with thirst and he reached out for the full glass that had somehow appeared on the table. He wanted it. He could smell the sweet malt and bitter hops, almost taste it on the back of his tongue. Harrison lifted the glass to his lips and drank.

His mobile's shrill ring pulled him from sleep, and for a brief second or two, Harrison had to pull his mind back into reality. He'd been dreaming in REM sleep and it was still dark outside, so he had to have been in bed at least an hour and a half. It wasn't morning.

He grabbed his phone. A number he didn't recognise.

'Hello,' his voice sounded groggy. His throat was dry, but it was water he needed, not beer.

'Dr Lane? Hello, Dr Lane?'

'Yes.'

'I'm sorry to bother you this late, but I'm told you're the man we need to speak to and that you like a fresh crime scene. It's Detective Inspector Richard Carrington. I'm working out of the Finchley area and we have an unusual murder. I don't suppose you might be able to come and take a look, would you?'

Harrison let out an involuntary deep yawn. His body was waking up. Even if he said no, he wouldn't be able to get back to sleep again for a while.

'Text me the address. I'll be there in about forty minutes.'

For a few moments, he allowed his sleepy brain to catch up with his conscious reality. He'd been out earlier with Jack in the Pig 'n' Whistle pub, which was probably why he'd been dreaming about drinking beer. He hadn't, of course; he'd stuck to his usual, an orange juice and then later a soda water and lime. They'd eaten, but Jack wanted to get home in time for his son Daniel's bedtime, and they were both tired after the busy week. He looked at the time on his mobile. It was a little after midnight. He'd gone to bed just after ten o'clock. Neither his brain nor body would appreciate being woken up like this, and he needed to get both back in gear before he got on his bike.

Harrison went into the kitchen and poured himself a large glass of water. Hydrating his tired brain would help and his throat was grateful for the fluid. He stood in the main living room of his Docklands apartment, looking out over the dark, flowing water in front of him. The Thames was a living being, catching the moon and city lights as it twisted and slipped along, heading out to sea and a salty oblivion. It was a clear night which would bring with it an extra chill in the air. Harrison concentrated on the flowing waters of the Thames, willing his brain to fire up and his focus to return.

Twenty minutes later, he was on his Harley, wrapped up and heading for Finchley.

The neat cul-de-sac of three-storey modern town houses was in a usually relatively quiet area of North Finchley, away from restaurants, shops, and pubs. Tonight, the neighbours were clearly enjoying being a part of a real-life crime drama, despite the late hour and the cold. A few were standing on doorsteps, chatting to uniformed police officers. Others pressed their faces to windows, indifferent to who could see them staring at the unfolding activity as their own cars became outnumbered by emergency services vehicles.

As Harrison parked his bike, he noticed one of the unmarked vehicles had a card in the windscreen. *Pathologist.* From this closer vantage point, he could see a very pale young woman with a blanket around her shoulders, sitting inside an ambulance with a paramedic. She was shivering. It wasn't difficult to diagnose that she was in shock.

'Can I help you, sir?' a young uniformed officer challenged him as he walked towards the house. Considering the lad was only about half the size and bulk of Harrison's muscular frame, he thought it quite brave of him to be the first to stand in his way. It wasn't long before another officer spotted the potential flash point and interloper, and joined his younger colleague.

'Dr Harrison Lane, Ritualistic Behavioural Crime unit. DI Richard Carrington called me,' Harrison reassured the officers.

The older man must have heard of Harrison, because he relaxed his stance immediately and a wave of recognition swept across his face, turning it from defensive to inquisitive.

'Dr Lane! Please wait here and we'll get hold of DI Carrington. He's in the house at the moment.' The officer spoke into his radio, relaying the message. 'He won't be long,' the officer informed Harrison.

Harrison tipped his head in response.

As they walked away, the younger man pulled his colleague aside and murmured in his ear, throwing a glance in Harrison's direction. It was a look that Harrison had received countless times as first impressions rarely matched preconceptions. Jack Salter described him as a man who looked better suited to being on the door of a nightclub that regularly saw trouble, rather than a psychologist with a doctorate.

While he waited, Harrison took the time to look around the area. The horseshoe-shaped group of houses each had an integrated garage and surrounded a small area of lawn in the middle. The road was wide, allowing for vehicles to be parked at the side without blocking access. All the houses seemed to have alarms, so it was likely some would also have CCTV or camera doorbells. The uniformed officers going door-to-door would be asking exactly this, along with whether anyone had seen or heard anything.

'Dr Lane', a man in a forensic crime suit, pulled the hood back and mask off as he exited the crime scene. Harrison estimated that DI Richard Carrington was in his forties and, based on his dark hair and eyes and tanned skin, had Greek or Turkish heritage. 'Thank you so much for coming out in the middle of the night like this.'

'It's fine.'

'It's a mess in there, I'm afraid, but I suspect you might be able to interpret what's gone on better than we can at present. It's like a scene from a horror movie. There's the possibility we're dealing with a random attack, but I don't think so. If you want to get a suit on, I'll fill you in on what we know before I take you inside.'

'Just the bare facts, please,' Harrison said to him.

DI Richard Carrington paused for a moment, considering Harrison's response, but then just nodded.

The detective had clearly been on shift all day. His morning's shave had been superseded by a dark shadow across the lower half of his face and his eyes were pink-rimmed with tiredness. The bright forensic lights, which Harrison could see beaming out through the curtains of the crime scene house, probably hadn't helped his tired eyes.

'An emergency call came in at five past eleven, from Deborah Milligan.' Richard nodded towards the ambulance. 'She had come home after being away for a couple of nights on a course for work. She lives here with her partner, a Lewis Ibbotson. When she went inside the property, she found him mutilated and dying. The place had been ransacked, and we've identified that holes were also dug in the back garden. It appears to have been a prolonged attack, although the neighbours claim not to have heard or seen anything unusual. By the time the ambulance crew arrived, Mr Ibbotson had died. He said one word to Ms Milligan, but it was so faint she's not entirely sure she heard correctly. He gave a name: "Caspar". She isn't aware that he knows anyone by that name.'

Harrison raised his eyebrows and nodded, but didn't say anything.

'Forensics have started, but obviously we need to be careful what we're touching as it's not all been logged yet. There are walking plates which will take you to the room where we found Mr Ibbotson and if you need to go anywhere else, just ask and we'll take measures. The pathologist is in there now, but he's pretty much done. We know when Mr Ibbotson died, and as you'll see when you get in there, it's pretty obvious how. What I need to know is why – and that's where I'm hoping you're going to help.'

'OK. I'd like as much space as possible please, so the fewer people in there, the better.'

'Understood. We'll need one officer present to verify that the crime scene hasn't been contaminated. That will be me, but I'll ask everyone else to give us a few minutes. Just be prepared. I've never seen anything this bad.'

While DI Carrington went back inside to speak to the team, Harrison suited up and started to prepare himself. He needed to shut out the surrounding bustle, clear his mind of the drive there, the last few fragments of his dream, and anything else which could take away his concentration. He closed his eyes and focused on his breathing, grounding himself.

By the time Richard returned and said they could go in, he was ready.

The first thing Harrison did was take another look at the outside of the property. It was three storeys, with one set of windows on the ground floor, and a single garage filling the other half. Up above, there were four more sets of windows, two on each level in uniform sizes; all looked doubled glazed, plastic frames and all closed.

Harrison walked up the path and paused at the front door. No signs of a forced entry. On the other side of the door, he could see two locks, and an alarm system panel next to it. It was idle.

Carefully, he stepped through the hallway on the walking plates laid down by the forensics team. There was nothing here to indicate what they were about to see; Harrison could smell it, though. The air was heavy with the iron-laden stench of fresh blood – and something else that was cloying and suffocating, a bit like boiled pork.

He entered a kitchen/diner that ran the full length of the house from front to back. To the left, a small dining table and chairs and the windows he could see from the street; and to the right, a fitted kitchen with patio doors to what he presumed would be the back garden.

Mr Ibbotson was sat in one of his dining room chairs, bound to it by coloured rope and tape. His blood was all around him, sticky claret-red pools on the hardwood floor, with small rivulets running along the joints of the wood. A machete, framed by a pool of drying blood and various pieces of finger, sat on top of the nearest kitchen unit. The butchered hand hung limply at the victim's side. It was clear that a fair amount of blood had dripped from it, but it wasn't his worst injury. His right arm had been severed from the elbow down, resulting in a raw, mangled mess of red flesh and white bone. You didn't need medical training to realise that nobody would be able to survive that amount of blood loss, not to mention the shock of the attack and amputation.

The man's face had been beaten; the extent of bruising and swelling suggested he'd suffered a prolonged attack for hours before death. His mouth was a dark-red, bloody gash, eyes almost sealed over with inflammation. Lewis Ibbotson had certainly suffered during his last moments on earth.

As Harrison moved towards the kitchen, the smell became overwhelming, turning his stomach, which was already unsettled after being wrenched from sleep.

The countertop held the clue as to why he'd been called. A large, elaborate golden star-like ornament sat pride of place, along with a small painted casket depicting religious scenes and a silver container in the shape of an arm. Human teeth, presumably from Mr Ibbotson as they still retained some of their former host's gum tissue, were scattered on the top of the counter.

Harrison looked closely at the gold ornament, then carefully opened the silver, arm-shaped box and the small casket to find them both empty.

He sniffed at a glass Pyrex bowl. It looked and smelled like it contained tea, with some small bones in it. Harrison recognised a finger knuckle. On the top of the cooker, something had been boiling in a large soup pan. The hob had been turned off now, but there was still a thin mist of steam rising up and filling the air with its putrid stench. He didn't need to look in the pan to know it was Mr Ibbotson's severed arm.

He could stand the smell of blood, but it was the cooking flesh which made him want to retch and took every ounce of his concentration to keep focused on the job.

He scanned the walls of the room. Photographs of what he presumed was the undefiled victim on various archaeological digs around the world hung alongside others of a smiling couple – him and Ms Milligan – in somewhat happier times.

Harrison stepped over carefully to the open laptop and small notebook on the dining room table. He had a strong suspicion what might be in the book, and, using the tip of his gloved finger, flicked through the pages. It was in code, but a rudimentary one that enabled him to see patterns – patterns that indicated that his suspicion was right.

Harrison turned and saw DI Carrington watching him from the doorway. He'd stayed silent, allowing Harrison to concentrate, but his eyes above the mask were expectant, questioning.

'What does his partner do?' Harrison asked.

'She's in marketing, works for one of the supermarkets.'

'Archaeology doesn't pay that well. Do you know how they can afford this?' Harrison nodded to the house around them. It was at least three bedrooms, if not four, and in a desirable area of London.

'No. She's outside. Do you want to speak to her?'

Harrison nodded.

'So, any ideas? We dealing with some kind of cannibalistic sacrifice by a religious madman? It looks like he's cooking up his arm to go in a lunchbox.'

Harrison shook his head. 'Let me speak with Ms Milligan, and I'll tell you what I can. First, I need to go into the back garden.'

'Sure. They shut the patio doors because it was starting to blow things around. The handle's been dusted for fingerprints, so just stick to the walkway and you'll be fine. You OK if I let the team back in here? It's going to be a late night as it is and they'll want to crack on.'

Harrison nodded.

He opened the door handle and stepped into the back garden with relief, breathing the cold early winter air deep down into his lungs, and out again, in an effort to expel the stench of boiled human flesh from his nostrils and body. He was surrounded on all sides by a high wooden fence and gardens beyond it. The back garden was only a small area, lawned and with flower borders, which had been dug up in three separate areas and the holes hadn't been filled back in.

Harrison dropped to a crouch and looked at the ground, using his phone torch light to study the footprints. For ten minutes he scanned the lawn and surrounding flower beds, looking on the earth for imprints. He couldn't see any tracks other than those which led to the holes; the killer hadn't escaped this way.

Satisfied with his findings in the garden, he re-entered the house to re-examine the kitchen. Two forensics officers were working, measuring blood spatters and taking images of the scene. He recognised one of the new cameras; it could take 3D imagery so that, later on, the team could bring the whole room back digitally and look at it again from all directions.

Harrison crossed to the kitchen units directly underneath the religious items and teeth. Carefully, he opened one of the cupboards and found exactly what he'd been looking for: a partial footprint – its pattern the same as the prints in the garden – on the bottom edge, and scuff marks inside, too. The cupboard was mostly empty except for a large wok and a chopping board.

'You'll want to log this,' he said to the forensics team and pointed at the footprint.

One of them stood up and came over to see what he was pointing at. Though her hood and mask hid most of her face, there was no missing the raise of her eyebrow when she clocked what he was pointing to.

'Thanks,' she said. 'Not looked in there yet.'

By the time she looked up again, Harrison was already on his way out through the door. He needed to speak to Deborah Milligan.

'HERE HE IS. Dr Lane just has a few questions for you, Ms Milligan,' DI Richard Carrington said as Harrison approached them in the ambulance.

Harrison smiled gently at the woman in front of him. She'd had a huge shock and would almost certainly never get the image of her mutilated boyfriend out of her head for the rest of her life. Her complexion was pale and grey. He could see the network of blood vessels underneath her eyes where her tears had washed away her make-up.

'I won't keep you long, I just have a couple of questions which could help us identify Mr Ibbotson's killer.'

She stared at him, pupils dilated, 'OK,' she barely whispered.

'Mr Ibbotson was an archaeologist, I understand?'

She nodded.

'Did he travel away often?'

'He goes on digs two or three times a year, usually for a few weeks at a time, and he's been writing a book in between. He's been going for interviews to go on other digs in the last few months, but they've only been short trips – a night away somewhere.'

'I hope you don't mind me asking, but do you or Mr Ibbotson have family money helping you with the mortgage?'

Deborah looked at him for a few moments, clearly contemplating not only the question but whether she should answer it. Then she shook her head.

'No. Neither his family nor mine are wealthy. He actually sends his parents some cash now and then. He gets good fees for his archaeological work and had a big advance from a publisher for his book. That's how we afforded the deposit on this place. He also got some bounty fee for finding something on his last dig; that paid him well.'

'You ran outside after you'd seen Mr Ibbotson, is that when you called the police?'

'Yes... I couldn't stay in there and I was frightened, so I came out here and called 999. But when the woman asked me if he was breathing still, I realised that I hadn't checked, and so I went back in. And he was alive. Just. I won't forgive myself for running out like that when he needed me. Maybe if I'd helped him he'd still be alive.'

'No, I'm afraid it would be very unlikely that you could have helped him. His blood loss was too extensive; I'm sorry.'

'I couldn't even hold his hand,' she replied, her voice crumbling into sobs.

He waited for a few moments while she regained her composure. She'd started to shake again, and the tears were flowing down her face.

'Did you have your back to the house when you were on the phone with the police?'

'I don't know. I can't remember. I think so.' She frowned, thinking.

'Was there anybody else in the close while you were out here?'

She shook her head. 'Not at first, but I think when I screamed for help, one of the neighbours came out. I'm really not sure; I'm so sorry I can't remember. It's all a blur.'

'That's OK, don't worry.'

'No wait... I vaguely remember an old guy, sixties, maybe older. He must have been visiting someone because he was walking out of the close. But that's when I turned and went back in to check on Lewis.'

'DI Carrington said that Lewis was able to speak to you before he died?'

It took her a few moments to speak again; the tears backed up in her throat, strangling her vocal chords. 'I wasn't sure. His voice was barely a whisper, but I think he said something like Caspar.'

'Thank you, Miss Milligan, and I'm so sorry for your loss.' He smiled kindly at her again and stepped away from the ambulance. DI Carrington followed.

'That help?'

'Yes,' Harrison replied. He was thinking hard and, for a few moments, the detective stood in front of him expectantly, waiting for some clue as to what was going through his mind.

'Are you familiar with relic hunters?' Harrison suddenly looked at DI Carrington's face.

'What, you mean like Indiana Jones?'

'Not quite, but similar. Religious relics have been huge business for centuries. Even as far back as the Middle Ages, there was a very brisk trade in them. Before the Reformation, it was believed that the saints were the source of miracles. If you were ill, or needed to exorcise a demon that was ruining your crops, it was the relics, the body parts of dead saints, that people believed held the power. Churches were competitive. Having a major saint in your church was big business. Worshippers would come from afar and they'd make a financial offering to the church in exchange for their hoped-for miracles. It meant there was a hot trade in stolen and fake relics, and churches weren't too particular about whom they bought from.'

DI Carrington was listening patiently to Harrison's explanation, but his brows were becoming increasingly furrowed as he waited for how this was all relevant to his crime scene.

'So is that what that box and other stuff are on the kitchen countertop?' he asked.

'Yes, and no. They're the reliquaries, the containers which house the saint's body parts. Nowadays, it's private collectors who are the ones paying for relics stolen from churches. It's still big money.'

The penny dropped for DI Carrington. 'Enough for a tidy deposit on a house?'

'Indeed. Unknown archaeologists don't get large advances for books, and I don't think they get bonuses either. But I also don't think Mr Ibbotson only stole from churches and archaeological sites. The most notorious relic hunter of the last thirty years is a man nobody has ever identified. He was like a ghost. Relics would disappear and no one ever saw who took them. That's why Interpol nicknamed him Caspar. But he's been very quiet for a couple of years. His last job was believed to have been in 2020, stealing a vial of Pope John

Paul II's blood from a cathedral in Italy. After that, he went quiet. That gold ornament in Mr Ibbotson's kitchen is the missing Pope reliquary, but the vial of blood isn't there.'

'So what are you thinking, that Ibbotson was some kind of dealer?'

'Possibly. Ms Milligan said he was making short visits around the country which could have been to connect with buyers, but he also had the opportunity to be a thief himself. Either way, it looks like he somehow double-crossed Caspar. The other two reliquaries in there were also believed to have been stolen by him. I think Mr Ibbotson was tortured first by Caspar, to tell him where he'd hidden them, hence the dug-up holes in the garden.'

'Torture – what by boiling his severed arm while he was still alive? That's extreme.'

'No. That came after. Once Caspar had dug them up, he realised that the originals were missing, and the reliquaries were empty. I presume that Lewis Ibbotson had sold them without their cases in order to avoid detection, or perhaps he was planning on doing exactly what his killer did in order to get double the cash. Caspar was harvesting Ibbotson's body parts to create fake relics. Without those, the reliquaries are virtually worthless. He was simply re-filling them.'

'Bloody hell.' DI Carrington shook his head. 'Nice piece of work that Caspar then, nothing like his cartoon namesake.'

'I think the notebook is a record of sales. My guess would be that Caspar was incapacitated for a while; ill, maybe – we have had a pandemic – or perhaps he could have been in lockdown somewhere. Mr Ibbotson somehow had or got access to Caspar's relics and has been busy disposing of them for his own gain, thinking he wasn't going to see him again. What you've got in there is payback. The knuckle bone is being soaked in tea to age it. The arm is being boiled to remove the flesh. Plus, Caspar was taking his victim's teeth – and who knows what other body parts he might have harvested if he hadn't been interrupted by Ms Milligan. One of the most notorious stolen relics is Jesus's foreskin from when he was circumcised as a boy, and said to be the only piece of him he left on earth.'

'What?' the detective exclaimed, open-mouthed, causing a couple of the uniformed officers standing nearby to look over at them.

'One was stolen in the 1980s, but there were at least a dozen churches which claimed to have it during the Middle Ages, so you can be sure that if they weren't all fakes, then most of them were.'

'So if Ms Milligan hadn't returned, he might have…'

'Who knows?' Harrison replied.

'I don't get why these things are worth so much that a man would do that to another human being.'

'If you believe they are going to help you, and you have the money, then I guess it's worth it to you. The non-religious do it with celebrity memorabilia. People will pay millions of dollars for items that have touched their celebrity heroes and heroines, just to get close to them. Look at Judy Garland's red shoes from *The Wizard of Oz*. They were stolen and went on to fetch millions at auction after being recovered.'

DI Carrington was reeling from everything Harrison had told him. 'Do we have any idea who this Caspar is?'

'No. But I would hazard a guess that the older man Ms Milligan said she saw walking out of the close was him. He was still in there when she arrived home. He hadn't finished and there's no escape route out the back. He'd have known that because he'd already been outside digging earlier. He hid in the kitchen cupboard, hedging his bets that she would do exactly what she did. Run out of the house to seek help.

Then he simply followed her out. There was always conjecture that he was some kind of acrobat or gymnast because of the way he could get into places that seemed impossible.'

'Surely he wouldn't have stayed in there like that. It was too risky?'

'This is a man who has calmly stolen relics from crowded churches and secure museums. He is a master at not being seen.'

'So we need to look into Mr Ibbotson's movements. Somewhere, he has linked up with this Caspar. I'll get in touch with Interpol, find out if there are any updates on our ghost friend.'

'He left behind a potential goldmine in relics. There may even be more buried in the garden. It wouldn't surprise me if he comes back.'

'Comes back here? Seriously? You think he's that brazen?'

'Like I said, I think he's proven just how brazen he can be on more than one occasion.'

'OK. Thanks for the tip-off. I can promise you that nobody, not even a ghost, is going to get back into that crime scene without me knowing about it.'

3

Harrison was staring at an image of a beautiful mermaid on his computer screen. She was lying across a granite rock surrounded by sea, posed on her side as though she was simply resting. She looked beautiful. Long blonde hair flowed onto the rock, and her silvery tail glinted in the pale winter sun. If it wasn't for the fact that Harrison knew the woman in the photograph was now lying in a morgue, and there was no possible way that human legs could have fitted into that fish tail, it could be a model posing for some fairy-tale fantasy photoshoot.

An overweight, pasty-faced young man in his mid-twenties burst into their basement office in a flurry of crisp packets and various pots of hot drinks and food. Ryan dumped the crisps and a coffee on his own desk, before heading over to Harrison's.

'One plain porridge,' he said as he put it down in front of his boss. 'You know the syrup one really is much nicer.'

'Too sweet for me; this is fine.'

Ryan didn't immediately walk back to his own desk, but

instead stood staring at the image on Harrison's computer screen.

'Tanya know you're looking at half-naked mermaids?' Ryan chuckled to himself.

His straight-faced boss raised an eyebrow at the mention of his girlfriend, Tanya. She was a senior forensics officer and despite Harrison's best efforts to stay single in order to focus on his work, the pair of them had become an item.

'She's dead; the mermaid, not Tanya.' Harrison qualified, taking him literally and always one to ensure facts were clear.

Ryan brushed it off. 'When you off to Jersey then?'

Ryan already knew that Harrison had been asked to go over to the Channel Island to help with the case. It wasn't every day that a mermaid turned up on British shores and police there wanted as much help as possible to get to the bottom of what was a highly unusual murder. The mermaid had made headlines across the world and she was everywhere on social media. The Jersey authorities wanted answers about who could possibly have done this and why. Harrison's reputation as the go-to expert on anything involving ritual or what their colleague, DS Jack Salter, would call 'funny business', meant they'd called on the head of the Ritualistic Behavioural Crime unit.

'Just waiting to hear on flights.'

'We gonna pack up the office before you go?' Ryan indicated the shelves behind his boss, which were loaded with books and various mementoes and relics of past cases. The dust had started to settle on the skull and ouija board directly to his right, and a small collection of voodoo dolls had obviously been knocked at some point and were now slumped on top of each other in the corner of another shelf. The bookcase contained all sorts of unusual and bizarre objects, most of which engendered fear and dread in anyone with an active imagination or strongly held beliefs. It was the reason why they now looked so dusty. The cleaners had left a note to Harrison saying that they would empty the bins and wash the cups, but they weren't touching anything on the shelves.

'I'll do it when I'm back. There's no rush to get out of here, and we can manage it all in one day when I hire the van and move you into your new flat.'

'Cool, OK,' Ryan replied. 'Any news on the new computers yet?'

Harrison looked at his assistant. He'd talked about nothing else but the high-end tech that he'd requested. The wage rise he'd also been promised had been gratefully received, but that wasn't what motivated Ryan.

'I promise you that we won't be moving over to the National Crime Agency until you've got your hands on every last bit of what you need.'

'Thanks, boss,' Ryan replied.

Harrison could tell there was still some reservation in his answer.

'I know change isn't easy, but going over to the NCA is recognition for both of us. We'll do it together.'

Ryan's smile broadened and he peered again at Harrison's computer screen.

'Not very Disney.' Ryan nodded at the image. It was a close-up of the mermaid, laid out on the pathologist's metal post-mortem table.

'Disney?' Harrison looked at him.

'Yeah, you know, *The Little Mermaid.*'

'Hans Christian Andersen wrote that. It was pretty dark and a fairly tragic ending if I remember rightly.'

'Disney did a modern Hollywood cartoon version.'

Harrison raised his eyebrow at Ryan.

'The girls at school used to like it. They had mermaid

lunch boxes and backpacks. You know?' Ryan looked at his boss's deadpan face and changed tack. 'I guess this dude was following the original story, then?'

'Mmhh, not sure yet what story he was following. You know that mermaids exist in cultures and folklore all over the world, don't you? They're not just found in Hollywood and fairy tales. In fact, they're quite often pretty nasty creatures, while others are worshipped like gods.'

Ryan hmphed in surprise, which Harrison took to be an encouragement to continue.

'In Cameroon, the Sawa ethnic groups believe in the jengu water spirit, and there's the Mami Wata who is worshipped in Africa and the Caribbean, and Melusine who is a European water sprite. In ancient history, the Greek Sirens lured sailors to their deaths. But it's not all history; I remember reading a research report about ten years ago that said workers on a dam in Zimbabwe were being terrorised by mermaids. They're believed to live in big lakes there. Most countries around the world have mermaid stories.'

'Well, Jersey's certainly got the best one now,' Ryan said, wandering back to his desk.

Harrison didn't reply. He wasn't sure that the authorities in Jersey were all that happy about being the centre of a global mermaid frenzy. It was one of the reasons he didn't have a flight time already. All the seats had been booked by journalists and media crews, or those who thought if a fairy tale could be true, then what other miracles might occur. So far, very little of the darker side of the story had found its way to the public. The police were keeping as much under wraps as possible while they worked out how to handle the investigation. It would only be a matter of time, of course. He needed to get over there sooner rather than later.

Harrison's desk phone rang. He picked it up, fully

expecting it to be someone from Jersey saying they'd sorted out his trip.

'Could I speak with Dr Lane please? It's Sergeant Callum Douglas from Harrogate police.'

'Speaking,' Harrison replied. He knew exactly what this call was about. The other week, a dying woman called Freda Manning had disappeared from a hospice in Harrogate and he'd reportedly been the last person to visit her. She'd since wound up dead in a house fire in London, along with her husband – allegedly. Harrison had known the Mannings as a child, and not only was he convinced that they'd murdered his mother and then made it look like suicide, but that the husband, Desmond was still alive and breathing somewhere and this was a plot to frame him and ruin his reputation. The issue would be proving it all because he also knew that Desmond was fabricating evidence.

'I'm following up on the disappearance of a Freda Elizabeth Manning from the PennyGate Hospice. I understand you are a friend of Mrs Mannings and visited her on the third of November?'

'I did indeed visit her, yes,' Harrison replied. He wasn't about to raise the officer's suspicions even more by telling him the woman was no friend of his and his visit hadn't been a social call.

'Were you aware that Mrs Manning had gone missing from the hospice?'

'I was told that was the case by a colleague.' DS Jack Salter had told him the minute he'd found out. He'd also told him about the fire, but that wasn't a piece of information Harrison should know, so he kept quiet.

'We need to take a statement from you, Dr Lane. There were no other visitors recorded after you left and so we have a few questions to ask you.'

'That's fine. I doubt there is much I can help you with though as I left her in bed and didn't see anybody else coming or going. I'm sure you have the CCTV.'

Sergeant Douglas simply replied, 'How about tomorrow afternoon?'

'That should be fine.' Harrison didn't let on that he might not even be here and they'd have to postpone.

They said their goodbyes, and he hung up.

Ryan was texting on his mobile, but at the same time watching him from across the room. He knew the full story and there was concern marring his usually cheerful face. Harrison said nothing and got on with working through his emails. He hated a fuss.

A few moments later, Ryan's mobile rang. 'Hi,' he said answering it and throwing a glance Harrison's way.

In the complete silence of their office, where no extraneous noise leaked from above to the basement corridors, having a private phone call was near impossible. Invariably, you could hear the sound of the person on the other end of the line, talking through the ear piece like some miniature person in a tin can. Ryan's current call was no exception and his need to have the volume up high due to too much loud heavy metal music in his teens ensured a private conversation was non-existent.

'He definitely going?' Harrison heard leaking from Ryan's phone.

Harrison looked up at his assistant.

'Tell Jack to stop stressing. I am going to Jersey. I won't hunt down and murder Desmond Manning. Yet.' Harrison looked pointedly at Ryan from under his eyebrows.

'Did you hear that?' Ryan asked Jack, who clearly had because Ryan got up and took his mobile over to Harrison.

'DI Salter, are you conspiring with my assistant?'

Harrison asked him. It was good-natured, but Harrison was a little annoyed.

'You know as well as I do that you're better off out of it until this calms down. Quite apart from the fact you're mixed up in two potential murder charges, a cold case review, and an abduction, you're not always the best at remaining calm in the face of injustice.'

'I am perfectly calm,' Harrison replied.

'Yeah? And what happens if we find where Desmond is hiding? Are you going to resist the urge to go and show him what you really think of him?'

'Whatever is going to happen will come to me in due course, Jack.' Harrison sighed. 'I'm not going to go to Jersey just to avoid Desmond Manning and whatever he and his wife brewed up. I will go because there is a young woman on a mortuary slab who has been butchered. I'm going to see if I can help find her justice. Desmond Manning will get his just deserts in due course.'

'I'd have thought you'd be on a flight by now.'

'I would be if half the world's media and every mermaid fanatic under the sun wasn't booking the plane seats.'

'OK. I was only checking.'

'I know. Thanks for your concern.' Harrison softened his voice. The little triumvirate of Jack, Tanya, and Ryan all had his best interests at heart and he knew they were watching his back. He just wasn't used to having anybody else involved in his life.

He handed Ryan his mobile back and was treated to one of his looks, which was a mixture between a mother saying you'd better behave now, and a teacher asking if he'd learned his lesson. Ryan returned to his side of the room and silence once more settled on their working environment.

Harrison knew things had returned to normal and Ryan

was no longer worried, when he heard a crunch come from his desk and realised he'd started on his new crisp packet mountain.

A few minutes later, an email popped into his inbox from Jersey police. His flight was booked for late afternoon today. He'd let Sergeant Douglas know when he was at the airport.

4

arrison sat at Gatwick Airport listening to the plethora of languages and accents around him. The bright-white fluorescent lighting in the main concourse made his eyes tired and dry. They'd already been struggling after last night's disturbed sleep.

He'd passed through Security and then walked the snaking temptation alley of duty free. He'd watched as other passengers succumbed, like Alice in Wonderland, to the 'Eat me, drink me and save money' messaging which whispered at them from each of the heavily stocked units in the rabbit tunnel. Seeing as he didn't drink, smoke or eat chocolate, it wasn't too hard for him to ignore their urging. At the other end, he'd bought only a bottle of water, a sandwich and packet of crisps from the WHSmith.

As he ate his sandwich, the rasping beep of a special assistance buggy slowly drove past to his right. Three children were sitting on the floor in front of him, chattering in French as they played with a model of a London bus. A baby squealed its displeasure at something in one of the cafe areas, its high-pitched wail cutting through the general airport hubbub; and the dingdong of the announcement Tannoy asked everyone to keep an eye on their luggage and not to leave bags unattended.

As Harrison started tuning out the surrounding sounds, an elderly man wearing a WikiLeaks baseball cap sat down in front of him. He clasped a folder with his printed itinerary and boarding pass, which he put away into an old blue holdall. He didn't look like the kind of man who used technology to uphold freedom of speech and whistleblowing. Harrison subtly watched him, intrigued. Perhaps a grandchild had given him the hat as a joke. The man made a call on his mobile, which was an old basic model, and not a smart phone; his accent was American. By the time Harrison had finished his snack and needed to head to his gate, he'd heard and seen enough to come to the conclusion the man was a fan of conspiracy theories. He'd expressed his surprise at having got through Security unhindered and was talking in whispered tones to whoever was on the other end of the phone. If he was really a whistleblower looking for anonymity, then the baseball cap might have been a bit of a giveaway.

Harrison took a quick look at his emails before heading to the boarding gate. A big part of him didn't want to leave. He wanted to hunt down Desmond Manning. He knew Desmond was still out there somewhere, plotting a way to make Harrison's life difficult. The whole situation made him angry and frustrated.

In truth, he knew Jack was right. He was better off not being around; he'd be a distraction if he stayed in London. Harrison had never relied on anyone before like he was now, but Jack had promised to carry on the hunt while he was gone. Besides, Harrison needed to help bring someone to justice for the murder of the young woman in Jersey. His needs had to come second.

There were no emails from Jack, which he took as a good sign, and just a couple from Ryan passing on a few enquiries from various different detectives. Ryan was showing himself capable of dealing with a lot of the basic ones, on top of his usual digital remit. Harrison was pleased how much his confidence had grown in the last few months. The move to the National Crime Agency was going to be good for both of them.

Harrison walked through the lino-lined corridors to the boarding gate, where a small carpeted area was filled with people. Some waited in line for the Jersey gate to open, others were already filing through its neighbouring gate to Inverness. For a while, the Channel Island and Scottish passengers intermingled, before a Tannoy called for the last passengers for Inverness, and a small wave of people rushed from various corners of the waiting area towards that gate.

Harrison waited in the far corner of the lounge, watching as passengers waved and chatted to each other as they arrived – evidence of the small community he was about to join. On the seat opposite was a discarded newspaper. The mermaid was still front-page news. This time they had a photograph of what they called 'occult symbols' painted on the sea wall at the beach where she'd been found. The supposedly informed tabloid journalist then went on to say that police suspected a cult was responsible for the killing. Harrison wondered if that was true or a complete fabrication to keep the story interesting. From what he could see of the symbols, they didn't look threatening.

He timed getting on the plane just right. Most people were already settled, including the two men on the inside seats next to him.

Most of the other passengers were either scrolling through their phones, watching downloaded movies, or reading the free newspapers that had been available en route to the gate. Harrison decided to take the time to rest. After his broken sleep last night, he felt more tired than usual and he needed to hit the ground running in Jersey.

The cabin manager informed them that the flight was only thirty-five minutes. Enough time for a quick power nap.

The aeroplane was pushed back from the gate, and the engines whirred into life. The smell of jet fuel drifted into the cabin before the air filtering system kicked in and the plane taxied to the runway, bouncing along the airport tarmac.

The man next to Harrison was watching some kind of zombie movie on his iPad. It was hard not to watch as the rotted corpse tried its best to eat a woman before being run through by her daughter. He mused to himself how incredible it was that despite centuries passing and technology, education and our knowledge of the world advancing by light years, humans were still sharing the same stories of revenants. Corpses that rise from the dead to terrorise the living. Interestingly, the living dead had become less intelligent with the passing of time. Zombies on the whole were rather stupid, whereas medieval revenants retained much of their living characteristics and intelligence. He wasn't sure what that said about modern society.

Harrison could just see past his neighbouring passengers as the bright green, red, white, and yellow lights along the runway come into view through the window. The plane came to a stop before the pilot received his all-clear and the engines roared and they sped up the runway, lifting off the ground effortlessly.

Harrison shifted slightly in his seat. His knees touched the back of the seat in front of him. For a tall man like him, there was very little space. He leaned back and got himself as comfortable as possible, closing his eyes. They stung slightly, tired and complaining about the dry air. He focused his mind on relaxing, shutting out the sounds of the other passengers, the rattle of the aircrew's trolley, and their questions whether people wanted a drink or some duty free.

He slipped into sleep for what seemed like just five minutes before the captain came on the speaker and asked the crew to prepare for landing. Outside was blackness, the sun long since gone down despite it only being just gone 6 p.m. He wouldn't be seeing much of Jersey as they landed.

They descended in the darkness and he could only tell they were getting close because he felt and heard the landing gear open and the wheels drop. Next, he saw the lights of buildings in the windows and almost immediately they touched down, followed by a huge back thrust as the pilot slowed their speed on the short runway. He had arrived in Jersey.

HARRISON MADE his way to the baggage hall, which was tiny in comparison to Gatwick and full of posters advertising various financial services firms. While he waited for the belt to start, he turned his phone back on. There was an email from the Jersey Detective Inspector, a Tracey Quenault, who had been liaising with him. A taxi would be waiting to take him to the hotel and she'd pick him up in the morning at 8:30 a.m. to visit the site where the mermaid was found and view her remains. Harrison decided that tomorrow morning would be a good time to avoid breakfast.

More than half of the plane had already left the airport building clutching their hand luggage and so the baggage carousel wasn't crowded. Harrison looked at his fellow passengers. A fair few of them were older, perhaps retirees returning from out of peak season holidays. There was also a small group who huddled together, looking interestingly at the other passengers. From their clothes and manner, Harrison decided they must be a media crew sent to this tiny little British island to cover the mermaid story.

It reminded Harrison to send a quick email to Sergeant Douglas from Harrogate. He didn't want the officer to make the journey down to London, only to find Harrison wasn't there. He pressed Send and pocketed his phone. While it had been Jack's idea to get away from the investigations about Freda Manning, the Jersey case had come in at just the right time. It annoyed Harrison that he almost certainly would have come to Jersey anyway out of intrigue; he didn't want anyone thinking he was running away.

The balding taxi driver who greeted him in the arrivals hall was a friendly soul who told him that he was a Jersey bean, which Harrison soon discovered meant born and bred on the island, with family here for generations. It didn't, however, stop him from moaning about a succession of things that he felt were being mismanaged, from the building of a new hospital to housing prices. When he stopped to draw breath and ask Harrison why he was visiting, the conversation then focused on the mermaid.

It was obvious the rumour mill was in full flow and his driving companion proceeded to inform Harrison that she had come from France, deposited there by French fishermen who'd been paid to dump her here by a mysterious mermaid cult that operated out of the Mont Saint-Michel area. It didn't take long for him to switch tack again and begin a tirade against the French fishermen who, according to him, were dominating the waters around the island and suffocating Jersey's own fleet. It was clear there was a somewhat testy relationship between Jersey people and their nearest neighbours, the French, who were just fourteen miles away.

By the time Harrison reached St Helier, and the Pomme d'Or Hotel, he'd already gleaned a flavour, albeit a rather subjective one, of Jersey society and the mermaid case he'd come to investigate. He suspected that his host, DI Quenault, would have a somewhat different view of things.

Despite the moonless night, Harrison had enjoyed the view of Elizabeth Castle as they'd driven towards St Helier. It wasn't far from the shore and lit up with enough lights to make it a dramatic scene. He was looking forward to daylight and being able to look around the island properly. Most of all, he wanted to view the so-called cult symbols that had been left, and the victim herself, to see if he could fathom out whether it really was the handiwork of a cult, or something entirely different.

5

DI Tracey Quenault pulled up outside the Pomme d'Or Hotel at 8:30 a.m. the next morning, right on time. It overlooked Liberation Square, named to commemorate the island's release from four long years of German occupation during WWII. Seagulls circled overhead, squawking and swooping at each other. The main road lay between the square and the yacht harbour, which even at this time of year was filled with moored boats, the rigging on their masts clanking in the breeze.

Harrison was already outside waiting, leaning against the railing that framed the two shallow steps into the hotel lobby. He was wearing jeans with a brown leather jacket on top and brown leather trainers on his feet.

DI Quenault, who was wearing a navy trouser suit with sensible shoes, was relieved to see he was dressed for the task ahead. Aged forty with shoulder-length black hair, she'd retained some of her summer tan. She enjoyed the Jersey sun and considered herself lucky that somewhere in her ancestry, her genes enabled her to tan easily and deeply. Mind you, she'd become more careful in recent years and was fanatical when it came to keeping her kids out of the sun. Factor fifty was the bare minimum. Skin cancer was not something you could ignore.

When she'd looked in the mirror that morning, even her tan couldn't hide the strain on her face; the case was already proving to be the most frustrating in her career. It had tired her out, but it hadn't knocked her spirit. Twelve years working in Manchester had nearly done that, but she was now older, wiser, and had a young family and husband to take her focus at the end of a long day.

She gave Harrison a big smile of hello. 'Dr Lane, welcome to Jersey.' She held out her hand.

'Harrison, please,' he replied, accepting the handshake and walking over to her car.

'How was your journey over?' she asked him as they got inside.

'Very short,' he replied.

'Yes, not much more than a hop over, really. Used to take me longer to get across Manchester than it does to fly from here to the UK.'

'Your husband from Jersey?' he asked.

She guessed he'd worked that one out from her surname.

'Yes. We met in the UK, but came here when we decided to start a family. It's a lovely place to bring up kids.' Her face darkened. 'Present situation excluded. It's usually fairly quiet here besides the usual domestics and the inevitable battle to keep drugs out.'

They both fell silent for a moment as she concentrated on reversing away from the front of the hotel. She caught Harrison's eyes wandering around the interior of the car and became conscious of the mess. There were the odd kids' toys littering the back seat and floor, and a scattering of various snack packets floating around or stuffed into the door pockets. The dark-grey mats were all covered in a fine dusting of golden sand. All the pool cars had been taken that morning.

'Sorry about the mess,' she said. 'Small children are not great when it comes to keeping things tidy. No matter how often I clean this car, I can never keep the sand out. One visit to the beach and we seem to take half of it home with us.' She smiled apologetically at him.

'Don't apologise, it's good to see family life.'

'You not got any kids?' She asked him now, her eyes leaving the front windshield and road briefly, to check out his wedding ring finger.

'No,' Harrison replied and looked out of the window as they passed Elizabeth Castle, the sand surrounding it revealed by the tide and glistening in the pale winter light.

She took the hint that this line of enquiry had been shut down.

'Shall I fill you in on what we know so far?' Tracey asked him, aware of the silence in the car.

'Let's get to the site where she was found first. It's important that I'm told as little as possible until I've made my initial assessment. It prevents bias and preconceived perceptions.'

She nodded, not sure what to say next. Dr Lane was a big man; not big like her father, with a belly that hung over his trouser top, but muscular and tall. He was handsome, too. A thick neck and a strong jaw. Definitely the strong, silent type. If she was picking a team for any kind of contact sport, she'd have chosen him from the line-up, for sure. Despite his size, he wasn't intimidating. Within his tough exterior she detected a kindness – although she wouldn't want to be on the receiving end if he didn't like you.

He certainly wasn't what she'd been expecting when her

boss had asked her to be liaison. Googling him had come up with absolutely nothing. The man had no internet presence at all. Pretty impressive in today's world. She'd been expecting a bespectacled academic type, but he was certainly a lot more distinctive. Her boss, Detective Superintendent Graeme Walker, hadn't told her much about him apart from the fact he was a psychologist specialising in ritualistic crimes, and he had a great reputation for helping in unusual inquiries. Their mermaid certainly qualified for that accolade.

As to whether he was going to be of any help to them, she liked to make her own mind up about people rather than take someone's word for it, and so the jury was out on that point. She'd worked with psychological profilers before and sometimes they could muddy inquiries rather than help them. There wasn't always a full understanding of the nature of police work with outside experts, but at least this Dr Lane was working within the Met. He should understand the territory.

Tracey decided to avoid the police talk and see if she could break the ice with her silent passenger. 'I think the population of the island has doubled with all the fuss this has caused.'

They'd just passed a TV crew standing on the top of the seawall along Elizabeth Avenue, trying to interview unsuspecting locals out jogging or walking their dogs.

'I've never seen this many journalists. We had to hire a hall for the press conference because so many wanted to attend. There are some who think it's good for tourism, but plenty of others who don't. Shame it hadn't happened in the summer when the beaches look better and the sun's shining. Might have been a better advert for the island then.' She found herself prattling on in the absence of any input from the man next to her, and wondered if he was on the spectrum somewhere, socially awkward, or just aloof.

Tracey noticed that the sun, which had caused her to squint just a few minutes ago, was now hidden behind ominously dark low clouds. They'd not been anywhere in sight when she'd left the hotel and they were heading straight towards them.

They'd left the Avenue, travelled through St Peter's Village and were headed down a hill towards a huge sandy beach which stretched as far as the eye could see. To the left of the beach was La Corbière lighthouse, which had featured in so many of the photographs posted online of the mermaid. They'd just reached the base of the hill when the rain arrived in big, fat sploshes on the windscreen.

'I live in the east of the island and we can leave our house in sunshine and arrive out west to pouring rain and high winds,' Tracey said, as if trying to excuse her home island for its unwelcoming weather. She knew she was also still trying to fill the silence, and it was making her self-conscious. Years of dealing with aggressive and abusive thugs had toughened her up, but silence seeped through the cracks like nothing else and soaked into her confidence.

She realised she'd said 'out west' as though it were some huge distance to travel. Seeing as Jersey was only nine miles by five, nowhere could be said to be far, but it was amazing how the island mentality had quickly taken hold of her way of thinking. Within a few months of being here, she'd started thinking twice about making the journey across to the west. In the UK, the distance would have been a daily occurrence. Nevertheless, with this side more exposed to the open expanse of the Atlantic, and the east protected by France in the Bay of Mont Saint-Michel, the two sides of the island had their own microclimates.

Tracey pulled into a dirt car park and turned the engine off. They were facing the sea, and the wind was buffeting the rain into the car, straight off the beach.

'Let me just check something,' she said and pulled her phone from her pocket.

Harrison said nothing, but continued to peer out through the water-smeared windows.

'We just need to wait in the car for about five minutes and this shower will pass over,' Tracey said, waving her phone at him. 'I live by this weather radar. It changes so quickly here, but you can see the clouds as they head towards us, and the one that's over us now is only small. It will be gone soon.'

Tracey decided to make another effort at small talk while they waited, keen to try to understand if she was wasting her time babysitting this man when she could be getting on with the inquiry. He seemed reticent to talk about himself, but had filled her in on the unit he ran and how he'd come to set it up. All professional, nothing personal. When that line of conversation ran dry she gave up and just sat watching the rain and wind hammer her car.

Within a few minutes, as predicted, the rain began to ease, and the sky brightened.

'There we go,' Tracey said, yanking open her door. 'All clear for around a half hour. I'll fill you in on how she was found.'

'If you don't mind, I'd like to get a feel for the place alone before you do that.'

He turned to face her now, his deep-brown, intelligent eyes looking intensely into hers. She could almost feel him reading her face, assessing her. It was slightly unnerving.

'No problem, you go ahead.' She sat back in her car seat and pulled her door shut. 'She was found on the rock to the left of La Rocco Tower,' was all she added.

'Thank you,' he'd replied and gave her a smile, which instantly warmed his face.

So he wasn't totally cold, just a bit of an unusual way about him.

She watched him get out of the car and go to stand overlooking the beach, and felt herself relax. She was back in her own space again. He seemed to stand there not doing anything, barely moving, apart from breathing in the sea air. What the hell was he doing? She didn't have him down as being some New Age spiritualist. They needed solid leads right now.

They'd already had around a hundred psychics from all over the world contacting the inquiry team. Some of them claimed to be in contact with an entire race of mermaids, others were more practical and talked about it as murder. They all gave different names for the killer or killers, and a huge variety of motivations behind the crime. Tracey wasn't about to waste any time following those up. She only worked off hard facts and evidence. Their victim was a young woman who'd been mutilated to look as though she was a mermaid. Whoever had done this to her was very much another human being, although perhaps one without much humanity.

Question was, would this mysterious Dr Lane prove to be any good at working out who had done it and what had happened?

6

Harrison had immediately recognised DI Tracey Quenault from the Jersey police website. Even if he hadn't checked her out on there beforehand, he'd have spotted she was a police officer despite her civilian clothing. He could instantly sense the tough crust that she'd developed in her career, and an innate ability to be able to handle most of what the human race presented to her without showing any reaction on her face. He clocked the wedding ring, the evidence of kids in the car, and her Manchester accent. He also sensed a little reservation in her approach to him. It wouldn't be the first time he'd met with that in this role.

He'd concentrated on looking out of the window, keen to get a sense of the island and those who lived here. She kept trying to make conversation and was clearly keen to find out more about him, which he managed to deflect.

He'd given her enough information to help her start forming some opinions. He explained how the ritualistic crimes unit had been his idea. He'd been helping a handful of Metropolitan police officers with some unusual crimes after they'd called on his expertise. Word had quickly spread as he helped solve cases that had completely blindsided them. Before long, he'd got the attention of more senior management and the suggestion came up that they employ him and the young computer analyst who helped him. Now he was off to the National Crime Unit because his services were being called upon by forces across the country. His visit to Jersey being a case in point.

'You parents must be so proud of what you've achieved,' Tracey had said to him, genuinely.

'They're both dead,' was all Harrison replied, and his tone made it clear that there would be no more discussion on that subject. Of course, it wasn't strictly true. His mother was dead, supposedly from suicide when he was eighteen, but he knew she'd been murdered. As for his father, he'd never had any idea who he was, let alone if he was alive or dead.

The conversation had served to bring Desmond and Freda Manning back into his head, and Harrison felt the tension return to his stomach. He wanted them out of his life forever. He needed to find him and end this, and it was frustration that welled up in him. Frustration that he was sitting in a car parked up at a beach in Jersey, waiting for a rain cloud to blow over, instead of hunting down his mother's killer.

As if the skies heard his frustration, a band of bright sunlight appeared from behind the black clouds in front of them, and the rain fizzled into finer drops, and then almost nothing.

He'd asked for a few minutes to himself, and got out the car. He needed to push the Mannings from his mind and focus on what he was here to do. He'd deal with them later.

Harrison walked over to stand at the top of the seawall looking out over the huge bay of St Ouen. It was a vast empty beach of golden sand which stretched in a gentle curve as far as he could see. The lighthouse was positioned on the tip of the left-hand arm, and to their right the beach rolled on into the distance. Directly behind them, on the other side of the road, were sand dunes and he could see a plane taking off from the airport, which was hidden up on the hill. La Rocco Tower was in front of him, around half a mile from the shore. Hewn from granite in another far gone age, its defensive walls told of a history where relationships with France were more seriously impaired than just some gripes over fishing rights.

He closed his eyes for a brief moment and breathed in the sea air. It was refreshingly pure, seasoned with salt and a hint of seaweed. From the sea shore, he could hear the waves rolling onto the sands. Harrison cleared his head, breathing deeply and grounding himself. When he was ready, he motioned for DI Quenault to join him.

She came alongside him on the sea wall, and he ignored her slightly bristly manner.

'Are you ready now?' she asked.

'Yes,' he said, turning to look at her and seeing the annoyance in the tightness of her lips. 'Sorry that I've held you up, but it's important to focus.'

That seemed to placate her because she immediately began recounting the events of just a few days ago.

'The initial report was made at just gone 8:15 a.m. You'll appreciate that the tides were different then. At that time, the high tide was about an hour previous. We're around two hours off the high tide at the moment. That's the rock she was on. Just to the left of Rocco Tower.'

'Who found her and how?' Harrison asked. The rock was

a reasonable distance away and it would have been difficult to see her in great detail from the top of the beach.

'Dog walker initially; she saw a light on the rock. That's what drew her attention – the killer had put a lamp behind the victim. The dog walker wasn't sure what it was, so didn't call emergency services immediately, but went up to the surf shop and spoke to them. They had binoculars, and that's when they all realised that it was what looked like a mermaid.'

Harrison nodded and looked along the top of the seawall for the surf shop.

'That's the surf shop over there.' Tracey read his thoughts and pointed to a painted shack on their right.

'Sea conditions were relatively calm that day, so one of the young surf guys decided to take a board out to get a closer look. They weren't sure at this stage if it was a real person who was in trouble, or some kind of model or prop, so they'd still not called emergency services for fear of looking like idiots. The surfer dude got to within a few feet of her and began to realise he might be dealing with a real person. He managed to get onto the rock to see if he could help her. Luckily they'd agreed a distress signal back at the surf shop and were watching him with the binoculars, so he motioned for them to call us, the coastguard, and an ambulance.'

'She was dead, I presume?' Harrison asked.

'Only just. When the killer or killers put her there, she must have still been alive. The surfer said he checked the pulse on her wrist and neck. Nothing. Yet she wasn't stone cold, and the pathologist put time of death at around the time she'd been discovered.'

'Risky.'

Tracey shrugged.

'How could the killer have got her there? Does the tide recede far enough to walk out?'

'Not totally. It does go a long way out, though. There is some CCTV and a surf cam along here, but nobody was caught on the beach. One thing we do know is that she didn't swim there. She'd have been too weak, and it was clear that she'd been carefully posed. We think he came in by boat, probably a small dinghy. Or we're also working on the possibility it could be some kind of cult within the surfing community, so they could have taken her over on top of a board.'

'Difficult to lift a dead weight out of a dinghy or off a board.'

'Yes, agreed. However, she was also lighter than you'd expect a grown woman to be because most of her legs are missing. We're also thinking that might be why we could be looking for more than one person. There's nothing to suggest it's a lone perpetrator.'

'How did the pictures start surfacing on the internet?' Harrison asked her, a thought forming in his head.

'The surfing community has an avid social media following. The minute word got out, the photographers were down here. By the time we arrived, it had already started spreading on social media. Unfortunately, it wasn't like your usual crime scene when you can restrict onlookers. She was there for all to see for a while until we were able to get out to her.'

'What about the symbols?' he asked.

'We need to get down onto the beach to see those.'

Harrison followed the stone steps down from the top of the seawall to the beach. He was careful not to slip on the pile of brown seaweed at the bottom and kept an eye out in case Tracey got into any difficulties. He hadn't wanted to point it out or offer a hand to her for fear of insulting her. As it was, she deftly jumped over it and the pool of sea water at the base of the wall, then followed him across the beach to where the symbols were clearly visible on the seawall.

'These have started to appear all over the island. The first ones were the night she was found here. We also got reports of some people dancing round a fire, like it was some kind of pagan ritual.'

'Mmm,' Harrison said, looking at the painted imagery daubed on the granite wall.

In usual circumstances, Harrison would use his tracking skills to assess a crime scene and work out what had occurred. That wasn't a possibility here. Quite apart from the fact that the sea would have washed away all the evidence, there was unlikely to be anything to view on the rock because the recovery team would have been trampling all over it, with anything else at the mercy of the elements. Sea water wasn't good for forensics. The only crime scene clues he would be able to glean would be from the body.

Instead, this morning he wanted to get a sense of the place. Why bring her here? There were other beaches in Jersey. And why now? What was the killer's agenda?

He watched as a lone woman walked across the beach and stopped at the sea line. She bowed her head and took something out of her pocket. It was difficult to tell what she was doing from where Harrison stood, but she seemed to sprinkle something into the water and then stand and stare out to sea for a while. If he wasn't mistaken, it looked like she was either saying a prayer or some kind of incantation. When something so out of the ordinary as this happened, it attracted all sorts of people. Some who saw it as proof of beliefs they'd held for a long time and others who just had an emotional need to believe that fairy tales and miracles could come true.

When the woman had finished, Harrison also walked

towards the sea line and turned round, looking at the wall and what was beyond. There were no houses directly on the beachfront here, just low-level restaurants and open car parks. He could see more buildings across the road, but in this particular area, the sand dunes were the immediate backdrop.

Could it be the tower?

He turned back round to look at the tower, just in time to see the sea creeping up on his feet. The tide slipped in fast, the beach shallow. He'd read that Jersey has the largest rocky tidal range in Europe, almost doubling the size of the island on low tides. This investigation had a lot to contend with. The sea wouldn't be an ally of theirs. It liked to protect secrets and hide evidence.

Harrison allowed the scene to settle into his mind some more, and then they walked away from the fast incoming tide and retreated up the stone steps to the car park. He made a mental note that when they got to the office, he'd look at the area from satellite imagery and see if he'd missed anything.

As they reached the car, a few splashes of rain hit their faces.

'Told you we'd get half an hour,' Tracey said to him. 'Good timing to head to the pathology department and you can take a look at our mermaid.'

Cadavers weren't particularly pleasant smelling at the best of times, but with the addition of a large chunk of dead fish, Harrison was glad he'd made the sensible decision not to partake of the hotel cooked breakfast.

DI Quenault was forearmed. She'd clearly sprayed perfume on her wrists for just this occasion, and he saw her sneakily take a quick sniff whenever she turned pale and thought nobody was looking.

The pathologist, Dr Imran Chaudhry, looked at Harrison. 'She's a lot better from a distance, isn't she?' he said, smiling and trying to make light of their discomfort. 'In all the photographs she's beautiful, but reality is she stinks and close inspection shows the flaws,' he added.

'Can you run through what you've found for the benefit of Dr Lane?' DI Quenault asked, and then stepped back slightly, trying to avoid breathing in near to the mermaid.

Dr Chaudhry rubbed his hands together. He'd clearly enjoyed the challenge of working out what had happened to the woman on his examination table. Harrison knew that it took a particular type of person to do his job; but every pathologist he'd ever met was in the profession to help speak for the dead who couldn't speak for themselves.

'Our mermaid is in her mid-twenties. Not sure yet where she's from, but we've sent various samples off for analysis and they should be back very soon. What I can tell you is that she didn't look like this a couple of years ago. She's had extensive surgery. Face tucks, body tucks, and lower ribs taken out to give her a better waist shape. I think our mermaid was probably a plus-size girl at some point. I suggest you get a cosmetic surgeon in to check, but I don't think that the work she's had done was carried out in a professional setting like you'd get in the UK. That suggests she might have had the work done abroad.'

He raised his eyebrows at this point and looked at them both pointedly. It was clear he felt this was a critical clue.

'So, what killed her?' Dr Chaudhry asked the question aloud, but immediately answered it. 'That's easy. It was blood loss and shock. He cut both her legs off and didn't stop the bleeding totally. Either he was incompetent, or he deliberately let her slowly bleed to death. After cutting the legs, he then sewed the fish tail onto her abdomen. Literally sewed it on, tucking what was left of her upper legs and abdomen inside the fish skin, from which the flesh of the fish had mostly been removed to leave room for the victim. The stitching was quite neat, actually.'

Harrison shook his head at the barbaric way in which the young woman had died. 'Would she have been awake?' he asked.

'Well, I can see that there was a sedative in her bloodstream. If I calculate the time between when she would have had her legs amputated and died from blood loss, and compare that to how much was in her bloodstream, then it tallies. She'd have woken up at some point undoubtedly, but how aware she'd have been I've no idea because the blood loss and shock would have taken a big toll.'

'I take it we've still no idea if she had been here for long, or maybe come over that night from France or the rest of Europe?' DI Quenault asked now from behind them.

Dr Chaudhry shook his head. 'Stomach contents, as you know, gave no clues. As I said, everything has gone off for further analysis, but it's wide open at present. There's more in my full report.'

Harrison stepped closer to look at the remains. He could see the area around her abdomen where the fish tail had been sewn on to her, and then further towards her back a scar which was the evidence that she'd had her skin pulled and tightened.

'How old do you think these surgery scars are?'

'I'm estimating around a year. From the rate the skin has healed and also the damage on the bones, you can see on the rib area that the damage is darker and healing has occurred. The legs, however, are fresh cuts to the bone made only just prior to death because they've not had the chance to heal.'

'Were there any marks on her skin, tattoos or cuts?'

'Nothing other than surgery scars. She'd had a boob job too, all within the same time frame. None of these surgeries would have left her completely without pain.'

Dr Chaudhry pointed to her left breast. 'You can see where there's scarring tissue, just tucked under here. Her breasts have been reduced in size and tightened so that they would have sat more pertly compared to her natural look.'

'Any evidence of sexual activity?' Harrison asked now.

The pathologist shook his head.

'None what so ever. She wasn't a virgin, but no evidence

that she'd had any kind of intercourse for quite some time. She's never had any children either. She's definitely not a seasoned sex worker. One other thing though, for a woman of her age, I'd expect to see a great deal more muscle tone. She had very poor muscle bulk, perhaps a consequence of the period of starvation, or possibly lack of exercise.'

'Or both,' Harrison said. He studied the young woman for a while longer. She looked so peaceful now, but the last hours of her life must have been torture. She'd been on every media channel in the world and yet she had no idea of her fame. Who would have done this to her, and why?

'You know that there was an item found inside the fish tail?' Dr Chaudhry asked him.

'No. What was it.'

'Totally bizarre really, considering everything. It was a small plastic walrus, stamped with the Horniman Museum.'

Harrison said nothing, he was thinking.

'By the way, she's half swordfish.'

Harrison and Tracey looked at Dr Chaudhry in surprise.

'The fish tail, it comes from a swordfish. Now, as far as I'm aware, we don't have too many of those around the Channel Islands.'

HARRISON AND DI QUENAULT were both relieved to get out into the fresh air.

'There were some items found with her. Are you aware of those?' Tracey asked.

'A lamp?'

'Yes, a simple storm lamp with a candle in it. She was also holding a mirror, and there was a bell.'

'What kind?'

'The bell was a small brass one, like you'd find on ships,

and the mirror was like one of those old-fashioned hand mirrors. They're back at the station; you can take a look.'

'Was she looking into it?'

'What do you mean?'

'Was she looking into the mirror when she was found?'

'Yes, it had been propped up so that although her hand was around the handle, it wouldn't fall over. If she had been conscious, she would have been able to see herself,' she replied. 'So, what do you make of it all?'

'I'm not sure yet. There's a lot of mixed messaging. You've got absolutely no idea of identity?'

She shook her head. 'She's not been recorded as missing in the UK, and we've contacted Interpol. I mean, she could be from anywhere, Australia even, for all we know. When we get back, we'll do a full briefing with the rest of the team, see if anything else has cropped up and run through what we have so far. Then you'll be up to speed.'

Harrison realised that DI Quenault was setting him a deadline. She wanted something from him either during the briefing or after. She was a hard taskmaster, but he respected her for that.

'Now, I need a coffee and something to eat. I didn't have breakfast because I knew we were going to visit Dr Chaudhry, and I'd like to eat somewhere other than the police canteen.' She smirked, knowing full well that Harrison had felt the same as her.

He could do with a bite to eat too, if he was honest. Something heavy to settle his stomach.

'We've got forty-five minutes before the briefing, so plenty of time,' Tracey added.

Forty-five minutes didn't sound very long, but then Harrison was used to traffic-logged London and not Jersey.

They picked up Tracey's car and drove for a couple of

minutes, heading towards the ferry terminal, before peeling off to the right and driving into an underground car park. She pulled into the first available spot and they walked up some steps to an open space in the middle of a modern development area.

'This is the Waterfront. Used to be literally under water once. All reclaimed land.' Tracey said by way of explanation.

Harrison got the feeling that she had given up on expecting him to provide conversation and was pointing out landmarks like she might do when taking her kids out on a trip.

They headed straight across the road to Coopers & Co cafe, which was half filled with a mix of people discussing business and women catching up with friends. The counter was stacked with cakes and sandwich options. Harrison chose a toasted cheese and ham sandwich with a carrot cake chaser. That had made Tracey's eyebrows rise. He also asked for a herbal tea, in contrast to her large cappuccino.

'Now I didn't have you down as a carrot cake and chamomile tea man,' she said to him as they sat down.

'Why not?'

'Well, I don't know, really. Just would have thought you were more a flapjack and espresso man.'

Harrison smiled, nearly even laughed at her cake and drink logic. 'Not sure what a flapjack man looks like, but I'd be happy to consume them as well. Just fancied the carrot cake today and I never really drink coffee or brown teas.'

For a few moments, they both smiled and relaxed at the final thawing of their relationship. Harrison could tell he was still on probation, but that never bothered him. He wasn't here to make friends; he was here to help catch a killer or killers.

When the food was brought over, they both tucked in.

The St Ouen sea air had given them an appetite which had only been temporarily ruined by their visit to the pathologist.

They'd just finished their food when a shadow fell over the table. 'DI Quenault, good to see you.'

Harrison could tell from Tracey's reaction that she didn't agree with the sentiment.

'Do you have an update for me on the mermaid? Perhaps I could buy you a coffee?'

'No thanks, Digby. You know the score. If you want information, you go through the proper channels.'

'Seriously? So you're no closer to finding out who she is and what went on, then? I've heard that she was still alive when she was found. That true?'

The journalist's eyes flashed at Tracey. He had stood himself in the only space between tables for them to walk through, effectively blocking their exit.

Her face was impassive – she gave nothing away. 'As I said, Digby. If you have any questions, you go through the proper channels. Now if you'll excuse us, we have to leave now.' Her voice was firm and measured.

Digby didn't look like he was about to just let her escape without at least one more attempt at persuading her to talk. Harrison, however, was eager to get to the station and carry on reviewing what the team had found so far. He didn't want to be late for the briefing and so he stood up from the table.

'Excuse me,' he said to the journalist, who was forced to turn his attention to the big man in front of him.

'Are you with the police?' Digby queried.

'I said excuse me, we need to leave now,' Harrison repeated and took a step towards him.

Digby threw a glance at Tracey, but faced with a muscular man mountain, he took the only sensible option and backed down, allowing them both to leave.

'I'll see you at the next briefing, DI Quenault,' he said to her back.

Tracey muttered under her breath.

'Bloody pain in the arse. He's been sent over by the *Daily Mail*, and is constantly on our backs so he can justify the jolly over here,' she said to Harrison.

Harrison was only half listening. He'd just remembered something, and he wanted to double-check if he was right before they got to the briefing. It might not solve the case just yet, but it was a clue.

8

_____

Since Maxine went, the girls had fallen quiet. They'd seen what he'd done to her – he'd made sure of that. He'd paraded her like a prize catch, ordering each of them to look and appreciate the beautiful creature he'd turned her into.

Maxine had been unrecognisable from the girl she'd first seen, but then, they all were. She had no idea how long they'd been here. With no natural light, it was impossible to tell when day turned into night. No external sounds entered their dungeon, so outside they could have been having fireworks for bonfire night, singing Christmas carols, or having a boozy BBQ, but they'd never know it. The only way they could get any kind of sense for which season they were in was by his clothes. From what she could gather, it was currently sometime in late autumn or early winter. Chilly outside because he'd put on a jumper and thicker trousers, but not so cold that he'd needed to layer up or wear chunky sweaters.

The silence was unsettling, and she wanted to call out to the others for reassurance, but she knew there was none to give. They were all wondering who was next and when it would be their turn. She didn't think it would be her yet. She'd been the fourth to arrive. It was Jennifer who had been there the longest after Maxine. Jennifer, who she'd heard sobbing while they slept. They were all losing the tiny fragments of hope that they'd clung on to.

In the early days, they'd whispered to each other from their individual cells. They weren't supposed to talk, but when he wasn't around, they'd reached out for human comfort and company in the only way they could. Telling each other about their lives, and about how they'd been persuaded to meet up with the man they now called The Jailer.

The place they were being held was a room about the size of a tennis court. Along one wall was a row of small metal cells, built from some kind of solid reinforced steel. They were impossible to escape from. Inside, she had a single bed with a bucket as a toilet and a bowl of water. He let them have books to read, but nothing else.

It was a well-organised set-up. Every day he would allow them out, one at a time, to empty their buckets and get fresh water to wash in. It was always cold. There was no hot tap here. Once a week they had to put their dirty clothes, which were blue hospital gowns, into a basket with their bedclothes and towel. He would collect them and then wash and dry them in the utility area on the opposite side of their cells. They were fed down here too, if you could call it that. It was always the same thing; sachets of some dieting shake that was supposed to give them all the nutrients they needed and nothing extra. It had the advantage of never needing a knife and fork so that he didn't have to worry about one of them turning the cutlery into a weapon to use on him. They never saw or heard anybody else besides The Jailer. Nothing of theirs ever left the room except down the toilet or sink. That was until Maxine did. She hadn't returned.

They knew she wouldn't because they'd all witnessed what The Jailer had done with the equipment which filled the rest of the room. It was an operating theatre and every single one of them had lain on its table many times, but none of them had endured what Maxine had. She'd heard her screams and then the high-pitched whine and groans of the saw. She'd known there was nothing she could do to help.

Instead, she'd lain on her bunk and put the pillow over her ears, desperately trying to escape the sounds. Yet they all knew it was just a question of time before it would be their turn because that was the contract they'd signed with The Jailer, however long ago it had been when they were last outside. Each one of them had signed the same terms and conditions. The trouble was, there was no get-out clause, there'd been no cooling-off period or returns policy. The second they'd signed, that had been the start of their living hell.

9

Harrison and Tracey arrived at the Jersey police headquarters with five minutes to spare. It was a relatively new building, just a few yards away from the tunnel which directly connected the east of the island with town and the west.

'I'd better introduce you to the boss,' Tracey said to him. 'He'll be leading the team briefing today.' She had thought things were thawing out between them, but he'd gone all quiet on her again in the car and seemed to be far more interested in looking something up on his phone.

They climbed the stairs, and she spotted Detective Superintendent Graeme Walker talking to one of her colleagues in the incident room. There were a couple of new faces this morning, drafted in from UK forces to help with the inquiry. There'd even been talk of whether they might need to set up an incident room somewhere else, in case they got too big for their usual space.

'Sir,' Tracey said, walking up to her boss. 'This is Dr Harrison Lane, from the Ritualistic Behavioural Crime unit.'

'Dr Lane, thank you for coming over at such short notice.' Graeme put his hand out and Tracey watched as Harrison took it and shook his greeting.

'It's an intriguing case.'

'Indeed. So damned intriguing we're really struggling. Never known a case like it,' Walker replied, sighing heavily. 'I'm sure DI Quenault has been filling you in, but we're about to start a briefing, see if there's anything new come up, so it's a good time for you to hear what we have so far and meet the rest of the team.'

Harrison followed Tracey over to her work station, where she pulled up another chair and motioned for him to sit. She saw his eyes go to the photograph on her desk. It showed a smiling, bearded man holding a toddler with one arm, and resting his hand on the shoulder of a little girl. It was the only personal item she allowed herself on the otherwise tidy desk. Her family took centre stage in her life, even at work.

The rest of the team huddled in towards the front of the room, sitting on desks or standing, as Detective Superintendent Walker turned on the smart screen. He was a robust man; Harrison could tell he'd played plenty of sports in his heyday – probably rugby based on his physique – and he still retained a healthy complexion and trim body. His black hair was now framed around his face with flashes of white, but he looked distinguished, rather than old.

'OK, everyone. We all here?' DSU Walker scanned the faces in front of him and seemed satisfied that he had everyone he was expecting. 'Right, first off, two new team members over from the UK. Detective Sergeant Alison Holmes and DS Lee Prentice. Plus, we have a ritualistic crimes expert, Dr Harrison Lane, who has joined us and I have high hopes he can throw some light on what we might be dealing with.'

Tracey threw a glance at Harrison, who didn't even show a flicker of reaction on his face. When she looked up, the new DS, Alison Holmes, was staring over at him. Either she had the hots for him, or she knew him. Tracey decided to make sure she cornered her afterwards to pick her brains and see which it was. While she could see that the handsome doctor might be an appealing sight to quite a few women, there was always the possibility she'd be able to find out some more about their mystery psychologist.

'Updates on progress, please. DS Le Scelleur, you were liaising with our French counterparts and Interpol, I believe.'

A detective in his forties, oval-faced with a receding hairline and a friendly demeanour, sat upright.

'Yes, sir. Making limited headway. There are no reports of anything remotely similar happening on the continent. Plenty of Satanists apparently, but no mermaid cults that have come to the attention of Interpol. I did, however, speak to the police chief in the Mont Saint-Michel region and they are going to make some enquiries. He seemed to think that there was a group of what he called "enthusiasts", who were wanting to hold a mermaid festival, but nothing as dark as what's been going on here.'

'Sir,' a uniformed officer spoke from further back in the room. 'Apparently there's been another religious or ritualistic offering left at St Ouen, close to where the mermaid was found.'

'What this time?'

'Well, he said a watermelon, a large shell and some white roses, amongst some other stuff. I mean, it could just be someone's picnic. It's different from before.'

'On a winter's day, sergeant? I don't think so,' Walker interjected. 'Does any of this mean anything to you, Dr Lane?'

'Quite possibly, I'd need to see them. Have they been recovered or left there?'

'They're on their way to us now.'

Harrison nodded.

'Make sure Dr Lane is able to view them as soon as they arrive,' Walker said. 'Dr Lane, what do you make of the graffiti we found on the seawall at St Ouen? Do you think it's some kind of mermaid cult?'

Harrison shook his head. 'I think you have a lot of people who have seen this as some kind of miracle, and others who have their own cultural beliefs, but I don't believe that the ritualistic signs I've seen, certainly so far, are connected to the crime itself.'

DSU Graeme Walker pulled his eyebrows together and sat down on a desk, focusing on Harrison. 'Can you tell us more?'

'Of course. The first thing to take into consideration is that mermaids aren't straightforward. There are mermaid legends in the folklore of most nations around the world. Many are seabound, but some are freshwater. Some of them aren't very nice at all and are evil hags masquerading as beautiful sirens. That's why at the moment it's not easy to pick the motivation behind the killing. As for the symbols, you have different people doing these for their own reasons. At St Ouen, it's what we today would consider pagan symbolism. Do you have it?' Harrison motioned to the board.

DSU Walker picked up a laptop next to him, searched for a moment and then a photograph of the graffiti on the granite seawall at St Ouen appeared on the big screen. He turned slightly so that he could view it and still see Harrison, who immediately continued.

'This one closest to camera is the symbol of water – an inverted triangle, which makes sense. The one in the middle is the Eye of Horus. It's an ancient symbol and again it appears in many cultures, but in ancient Egypt where it originates, it would have been painted onto fishermen's boats to protect them from harm. Finally, the symbol furthest from camera, which looks like a one-legged figure, is the ankh, representing eternal life. All of these are protective rather than evil. They might have been put there by some well-meaning individual or group to protect the soul of the young woman who is in the morgue right now. Or perhaps to protect the island from her or whatever killed her.

'I think it's likely that once it was realised the media were interested in this artwork, others, probably youths and young adults, thought it would be fun to splash them around town too. The ones that I've been shown elsewhere on the island are random; there's no meaning to them or their configuration, and they're not well drawn. If this was a cult that had committed the murder, then they've proven themselves to be highly organised. Therefore, the random symbolism doesn't fit with that.'

The detective superintendent dipped his head, thinking deeply. 'We've certainly seen a lot of interest in this, so it makes sense that there will be third parties getting in on the action, but what about the crime itself?'

Harrison sighed and shook his head. 'I'm still formulating a full profile, but in my view it's not a cult behind it either.'

DSU Walker tipped forward and raised his eyebrows, urging Harrison on.

'Whoever did this put a huge amount of effort into it. This has taken precision planning and that came from a very personal and strongly held motivation. A cult could be highly motivated, but they would be more clinical, more ritualistic. This has the hallmarks of something more personal.'

'OK, thank you, Dr Lane, once you've had a chance to

become fully acquainted, please share the full profile with us.' DS Walker looked up and addressed the room. 'We still don't know whether we're dealing with one person or a group. We don't even know if they are in Jersey. She could easily have been brought over from France under the cover of night. But why choose our island to stage the macabre scene, I don't know.'

He looked back at Harrison and then to his team. 'We have to keep our minds totally open. The only thing we do know is that the victim isn't somebody who has been reported missing here, which suggests she's originated off island. What else we got?'

Detective Superintendent Graeme Walker sighed and looked at the faces in front of him. 'Who was looking into the objects found with the victim?'

'That's me, sir,' a curly-haired man in his thirties stood up from his desk.

'OK, DC Edwards, what have you got?'

'Sir, the hand mirror is an antique, probably 1950s. I've spoken to a dealer here, and she told me that you can pick them up in charity shops for next to nothing, so the chances of tracing ownership are going to be slim to zero. Same deal with the bell, I'm afraid. As for the plastic walrus, we know it's from the Horniman Museum, but they sell hundreds of the damned things every year. We're unlikely to be able to trace him that way, although when we catch him, we might be able to prove he visited there sometime, which gives us a UK link.'

'I want the mirror and bell photographed and released to the media. See if anyone recognises them. Get them across to France too. They've a ton of flea markets over there for collectables and antiques. What the hell the walrus is all about, I've no idea; perhaps it means something to either the killer or victim.'

'If I may?' Harrison spoke again.

'Dr Lane, please do. Any input is considered.'

'I think the museum does have a connection, but it's probably more to do with what the killer has done, rather than who they are. One of the most famous exhibits at the Horniman Museum, besides an over-stuffed walrus, is what was once thought to be a dead mermaid.'

Everyone in the room was looking at him now, intrigued.

'You've probably heard of the American showman, P.T. Barnum, who had a circus that included people who were labelled "freaks", and a museum of curiosities that was actually full of hoaxes. The Fiji mermaid was one of those hoaxes, quite an ugly thing really, but it inspired others, and there is one that is now an exhibit at the Horniman. What makes it relevant here is that, of course, it was no mermaid, but a fake made up from parts of a fish, chicken claws, wood and papier-mâché. I think it's a nod from one imitation mermaid creator to another, and Mr Barnum's original hoax.'

'You think this is some kind of barbaric joke?' Walker asked him.

'No, definitely not a joke. It's obvious from what I've seen already that the killer takes his creation incredibly seriously. It's more a sign of respect. Perhaps even the inspiration.'

There were a few murmurs around the room at this.

'It could also make it more likely that our killer is from the UK as the Horniman is in London,' Walker added. 'I appreciate you've only been with us one morning, Dr Lane, but are there any other observations you want to share at this point?'

'The one thing I would say categorically is that they would

have been there watching. Somewhere along that beach, or in the dunes maybe, they were watching her discovery and the reactions of those who found her. Look very closely at who was there. Did anyone notice someone who was perhaps not taking part in the rescue process, but looking on? Maybe someone drove past them on the headland if they were using a telescope or binoculars. They wanted her found. We can see that by the use of the lamp. They will also be revelling in the attention she's receiving. That's evident in the meticulous detail and careful positioning of her.'

'Right, can someone pick up on that, please? Let's go through all the eyewitness statements again and see if anyone remembers someone hanging around. Go check on any residences in the area. Put a statement out to the media with the mirror and bell photos and ask if anybody saw someone acting unusually in that area.'

DSU Walker paused a moment. 'So what about our victim, any progress?'

Tracey spoke up now. 'Nothing, boss. Nobody has responded to the media attention and said they recognise her. Her DNA and fingerprints aren't coming up on any databases, including the missing persons one in the UK or in Europe. We've definitely not got anybody matching her description reported as missing here – and before anybody wise cracks,' she said to the room with an eyebrow raise, 'I mean description prior to getting a tail.

'We're getting a mock-up of what she might have looked like prior to all her surgery, in case people are just not recognising her as she is, but definitely no matches on the database for DNA. There's a cosmetic surgeon arriving tomorrow morning. He should be able to tell us what kind of standard of surgery she had and maybe track it to where. Could be an East European back street job. Apparently, it takes about fourteen years to train to be a cosmetic surgeon – no wonder they charge so much.'

'Hoping for a freebie tomorrow,' someone shouted from the back, and a ripple of laughter went round the room.

'Yeah, yeah, very funny.' Tracey smirked back at her heckler, totally unfazed. It served to break the tension in the room – something they could all do with.

'That's if the killer wasn't responsible for it all,' Harrison said.

The room fell silent again.

'What do you mean, Dr Lane?' Walker asked him.

'How do we know that all the surgery wasn't carried out by the killer? All part of his creation?'

'But that would mean he'd have had to have held her captive for at least a year?'

Harrison nodded.

'It's a specialist skill,' Tracey said to him.

'It is, but, as we've also all said, the standard of work wasn't the best.'

'I think it's something we can add to our list of possibilities,' DSU Walker said now.

'What about the swordfish?' Walker addressed the room again.

'We've sent samples off to a fish expert in London. They're going to let us know where they think the fish might be from. Unlikely to have been caught around here, although not totally impossible,' DC Edwards answered again.

'OK, if there's nothing else, let's get back to it.'

The briefing dissolved as everyone returned to their workstations. Tracey pointed Harrison to a spare desk and screen, and he immediately logged on and started reading through all the statements that had been taken. He declined her suggestion of a tour of the police station to find the canteen.

She'd just settled back down at her own desk when she spotted the UK detective, Alison Holmes, get up and head out the door which led to the toilets. Tracey jumped up. Now was a good time to be nosey; besides she needed to go too. The coffee earlier had worked its way through her system.

DS Alison Holmes was in a cubicle by the time Tracey reached the ladies' toilets, and rather than risk missing her if she too went into one, she decided to wash her hands and try to tidy herself up after the windswept beach. It was only right that she made contact with the officer, anyway. Show her that they're a welcoming bunch.

Tracey looked in the mirror and found herself sighing at what she saw there. The dark circles under her eyes were more than evident and her skin looked dry and lined. Maybe she should talk to the cosmetic surgeon about a discount. She was running her fingers through her sea-tangled hair, when Alison exited and headed to the sink beside her.

'Hi.' Tracey smiled warmly at her. 'Welcome to Jersey. When did you get here?'

'Thanks. We arrived yesterday.'

Tracey saw the woman's eyes drop to her ID, hanging around her neck.

'DI Tracey Quenault,' she said, introducing herself, but refrained from holding her hand out because Alison had hers under the tap.

'DS Alison Holmes,' the younger woman smiled and replied, albeit unnecessarily.

'Where you from?' Tracey questioned.

'The Met. I work out of the Kensington area usually. This case sounded interesting and I've never been to the Channel Islands before.'

Tracey gauged her to be in her late twenties, pretty, with a mixed ethnic heritage.

'You might know Dr Lane then, he's Met police,' she fished.

'I've never met him, but heard about him,' the young woman replied. 'He's got an incredible reputation. You know that he can track as well?'

'Track?'

Alison was drying her hands on a paper towel as she talked and turned to give Tracey her full attention.

'Yeah, you know, follow trails and see where people have walked and stuff. He was brought up by a Native American tracker, pretty awesome.'

'Wow, you'd never have guessed that from a psychologist.'

Alison smiled and raised her eyebrows. 'No. He's quite unusual and so knowledgeable. He'll help you catch the mermaid killer, for sure. If he suggests something, I'd listen.'

'I'm sure he will help,' Tracey replied, avoiding the suggestion, which she presumed was referring to what he'd said in the briefing. 'And if there's anything you need, or don't know where something is, just ask. We're a friendly bunch here.'

'Cheers.' With that, Alison exited the toilets.

Behind her, Tracey's interest in the man of few words, Dr Harrison Lane, had been heightened; she hoped he really was as good as his reputation suggested.

10

Harrison spent the rest of the afternoon going through all the statements and evidence that had been collected on the day the mermaid was found. This stage of an investigation was always tiring work because it involved taking in huge amounts of information in order to process it and come up with a clear idea of what had gone on. His eyes grew dry and scratchy from scanning document after document, and when the 'offerings' from St Ouen arrived in the building and he was able to look at them, it was a welcome break.

They were pretty much as had been described. A watermelon, conch shell, and some white roses. They'd been wrapped in a blue cloth. Eyewitnesses reported seeing a small group of people at the water's edge, acting strangely. Then they threw the wrapped-up items into the sea and left. They'd clearly not figured out the tides though because within twenty minutes, the blue cloth and its offerings had beached and were picked up by a woman who'd been collecting driftwood and witnessed the whole thing.

Knowing what had gone on just a few days previous, she did her civic duty and called it in to the police.

'Don't suppose she took any photographs of the group, did she?' DI Quenault asked the PC who handed over the evidence.

'Unfortunately not. She called us from home, took the items back with her because she hadn't taken a mobile phone along.'

'Any clues as to who they were?'

The young officer withdrew a notebook from his pocket. 'The lady said that they were a group of three men. Ages ranged from mid-thirties to mid-forties. She said they were speaking French and appeared to be saying a prayer before they threw this lot in.' He gesticulated at the bagged-up items in front of him.

'She suggested that they looked like fishermen. I pressed her on what a fisherman looks like, what gave her that impression, and she said they had weathered skin, healthy complexions and wore sensible waterproof clothing.' He looked up at Tracey at this point and shrugged his shoulders. 'I could see where she was coming from on that, although I appreciate it's not much of an ID to go on.'

'Next thing she'll be telling us that one of them was probably called Pugwash,' Tracey replied with joking sarcasm in her voice.

'Pugwash? Who's that? Is he French?' The young PC looked bemused.

'Never you mind, you're too young. She say anything else?'

'Not really. Just that they were acting a little oddly.' He looked up at Tracey, checking her face for any sign of what she thought of his report.

'OK. Thanks for bringing these up.'

He nodded, and, with a quick glance at Harrison, turned and left.

'I'm wondering if they're our French mermaid cult connection,' Tracey said to Harrison.

He shrugged his shoulders, and she picked up the message that he didn't agree.

'It's possible. Remember, we have to keep our minds open. It could even be that they've just come across her and for some reason didn't want to go back to port with her so they dumped her here.'

Harrison shook his head. 'No. She was deliberately staged, and she hadn't been in the water. There was too much attention and care put into it. She wasn't dumped.'

'Yeah, you're right about that. I'm clutching at straws. We're keeping a close eye on the comings and goings at the harbour, so I'll get someone to look into whether a French boat with three men has been here for a while or if it maybe arrived today. Could still fit with the theory it's some mermaid-obsessed group from the continent.'

'Mmmh,' Harrison replied. 'The offerings are the kind of things that someone who worshipped Mami Wata would give to the sea.'

Tracey looked at him as though he'd just brayed like a donkey. 'Come again?' she said.

'Mami Wata is an African water spirit who is also vener-ated in the Afro-Caribbean communities and diaspora around the world. It's not a cult, it's a spiritual belief; she's a deity, and she's half woman, half fish. Just like our mermaid. Her followers believe she will give them wealth and good health. She's often depicted holding a mirror.'

'Then that does fit with our Jersey mermaid.'

'There are similarities, but like I said earlier, there are lots of mermaid stories around the world. They're similar, but different.'

'Even with this?' Tracey gesticulated at the offerings in front of them.

'Our mermaid is blonde, white-skinned and blue-eyed. That doesn't fit with an African Mami Wata.'

'So maybe they were improvising.'

'A lot of effort has gone into creating her. If their aim was to venerate Mami Wata, don't you think they'd have chosen a Black woman as their target?'

'Maybe they're just not racially motivated,' Tracey mumbled. Harrison was treated to a small insight into what her daughter might look like when she wasn't getting her own way.

'How many people have arrived in Jersey wanting to see the mermaid or hoping to see another one? This story has gone global. Just because three men turn up on the beach and make an offering, doesn't necessarily connect them to her killer.'

'I realise that,' Tracey replied, the annoyance in her voice. 'But we've got nothing to go on, so at least this could be a potential line of enquiry.'

Harrison shook his head and looked at the evidence again. 'I don't think they're our killers.'

'With all due respect, I think you need to tell the boss about this and let us decide if it's relevant to the inquiry or not.'

'Fine,' Harrison replied. He wasn't going to carry on arguing now. He could tell he'd annoyed her, and he didn't want some petty disagreement taking his concentration away from this investigation.

'Can I see the other things that were found with her?'

Tracey looked at him from under raised eyebrows.

'I just need to see if they're connected to Mami Wata or any other kind of mermaid folklore.' Harrison stood firm and folded his arms across his chest.

'OK, I'll introduce you to the evidence team.'

TEN MINUTES LATER, Harrison was looking at the mirror and bell that had been found with their mermaid. He was impressed with the efficiency of this place. A request like that would have taken three or four times as long at somewhere like Lewisham, but he guessed that was down to their size. This was the biggest case Jersey's small force had dealt with in a few years, so it was clearly being prioritised.

The mirror was an old-fashioned brass mirror, quite plain, and as DC Edwards had said in the briefing, a quick look on eBay confirmed there were plenty of them available for just a few pounds. For a moment Harrison allowed himself to be distracted by the thought that Tanya might appreciate one of the better-quality ones for Christmas. There were some lovely art nouveau ones for less than fifty pounds.

He pulled himself up with a start. This was exactly the reason why he'd tried to avoid relationships. They invaded his concentration. He gave himself a mental slap and pushed away the image in his head of Tanya sitting looking in the mirror. Focus was everything.

Harrison looked back at the mirror. For the detectives, their only hope would be seeing if they could trace a previous owner in Jersey, as Walker had suggested. For Harrison, though, it added to what he'd been thinking about the motivation behind the killing.

The bell was a small brass one, again vintage and with a rope hanging from its clanger. It was the kind that was often seen described as a ship's bell and used in pubs to ring last orders. It too was plain, with no distinguishing features, so was going to be hard to track ownership. More to the point, what was its significance? Harrison could understand the mirror, but why the bell? It couldn't be physically used to attract attention like the lamp, because it was just found lying next to her, so it had to be symbolic.

The lamp was modern. One of the reproduction storm lamps you can buy at garden centres. It wouldn't have been cheap because of its size, but they were readily available. The team were trying to track down which shop it had been bought from as that would give them an idea of where the killer might be from, and potentially some CCTV or bank records of them buying it.

Some ideas were forming in Harrison's head, but he still didn't feel as though he'd come close to working out the killer's – or killers' – motivations yet. There was something in the back of his mind that he wanted to check out and, for that, he needed a book.

He tracked down Tracey, who, thankfully, appeared to have already moved on from their earlier altercation. She was one of those people who became passionate about something in the split of a second, but equally could move on from it just as quickly. The latter trait, Harrison thought, was a healthy one.

'Can you tell me where the nearest library or bookshop is?' he asked her.

'We boring you already? After some holiday reading?' she said to him.

He could tell she was joking, but at the same time he could also tell she was inquisitive, which was, after all, an essential characteristic of a detective.

Tracey directed him to town where the nearest bookshop was a Waterstones.

The walk into town was a welcome break. It had been easy to find the bookshop at the top end of the main shopping area, on Queen Street. The double-front windows of Waterstones were piled high with books ready to entice the Christmas shoppers. Plus, there was a variety of book spin-off merchandise such as cuddly Gruffalos and Peter Rabbits, and an entire section of Harry Potter memorabilia, which made the window display look fun and interesting for passers-by who might not be interested in just words.

Harrison was into books. He didn't get to read anywhere near as much as he'd like to, apart from academic research and information relating to his ritualistic knowledge. Keeping up with changing trends in world religions and newly formed cults and practices kept him busy, for the most part. He missed reading a good book, though. Nothing like getting invested in an interesting character and story, which, with some good writing and an active imagination, could be helped off the page and into his head. Not today, though. He was going to buy a book, but it was for the investigation, not his own pleasure.

Harrison walked through to the back of the shop where he could see the kids' section was packed high with all sorts of cuddly characters and brightly covered books. The difficulty was knowing where he'd find what he wanted.

'Can I help?' A young woman in dungarees and with long hair and tattoos was smiling up at him. He had obviously looked lost.

'Yes I'm trying to find a copy of *The Little Mermaid*,' he said to her.

'No problem, that's over here.' She started to walk away,

leading him towards a brightly coloured section that sported the Disney logo.

'Not the Disney version,' Harrison qualified. 'I want the original by Hans Christian Andersen.'

'Ooh, that's dark,' she said, widening her eyes. 'Most parents don't like reading his stories to their kids anymore, too worried they're going to psychologically scar them, but it never did us any harm, did it? I'm afraid you'll have to buy his complete book of *Fairy Tales* because it's only a short story and so we don't have a separate book for it. Apart from the modern retellings, of course. Totally sickly sweet if you ask me,' she added.

Harrison hadn't asked her, but he imagined he'd agree with her. 'That's fine,' he replied, following in her wake. She walked straight up to a shelf, reached out and handed him a copy of Andersen's *Complete Fairy Tales*.

'Thank you,' he said, smiling at her. She clearly loved her job. She was in her element, surrounded by books. A good place to be in life.

The man at the till was a little older, but just as friendly. 'Are you collecting the points?' he asked Harrison, who shook his head. He couldn't be bothered with all the retail loyalty schemes.

With his big book of Fairy Tales safely secured, Harrison decided to head back to his hotel and some dinner. Somehow he'd forgotten to eat lunch and his toasted sandwich and carrot cake brunch was a long, distant memory. He hadn't fasted for a few days, and his body was missing the feeling of lightness and energy it gave him; but today, with the fresh air and with being away from home, he needed food.

. . .

HARRISON CHOSE room service for dinner. A busy day meeting lots of new people and with information overload in his head meant he just needed to be alone and have some quiet. He wanted something that would be easy to eat, so opted for a burger and fries.

As usual, he didn't bother to turn on the TV, just relaxed back on the bed and opened his new book acquisition.

At about 8 p.m., his mobile rang. It was Tanya trying to WhatsApp video call him.

He accepted and was rewarded by the vision of his beautiful brunette girlfriend, sitting on the sofa in her flat and smiling.

They chatted about their days. It wasn't the usual conversations that couples have. The nature of their work meant it was decidedly darker than your average *How was your day?* chat. As a senior forensics officer, Tanya had been helping with a double murder at a pizza restaurant. Two young men who'd met their deaths in what was almost certainly an argument related to drugs crime.

'How you finding it in Jersey?' she'd asked him.

'It's fine. Early days,' he'd replied.

'What are the team like? You are making an effort to talk to people and not being Mr intense, aren't you?'

Harrison wasn't entirely sure what she meant. 'I have to be focused on the work. If I'm not, then I'll miss something. I'm getting on fine with the team,' he replied, choosing to forget about the near altercation with DI Quenault earlier.

Tanya didn't look totally convinced, but she let it go.

'What you reading?' she asked. She could see the book lying on the bed beside him.

'Hans Christian Andersen's *Fairy Tales*.' He smiled, holding the book up to his phone camera.

'What! Why? I know you deal with some strange folklore at times, but aren't fairies pushing it?'

'It's for "The Little Mermaid" story.' He smiled back at her again.

'It's pretty depressing stuff,' he said to her, 'She basically gave up being a mermaid because she fell in love with a prince she'd rescued,' Harrison continued. 'But she had to give up her voice and every time she walked, it was like knives going into her feet. She had to persuade him to marry her or she would die on his wedding night if he married someone else, and, because she had no soul like a human, she'd dissolve into sea foam.

'He treats her like a favourite dog, so it's very un-feminist, and then he does fall for someone else: a princess he mistakenly thought saved him. So her sisters go to the evil sea witch to get her help.

'Listen to this: "We have given our hair to the witch, said they, to obtain help for you, that you may not die tonight. She has given us a knife: here it is, see, it is very sharp. Before the sun rises, you must plunge it into the heart of the prince; when the warm blood falls upon your feet, they will grow together again, and form into a fish's tail, and you will be once more a mermaid." Nice solution, just stab the man you love. Quite scary stuff, don't you think for a bedtime story?' Harrison said to Tanya, looking up from the book to see her response.

'I liked you reading me a story,' she said to him, flirting with her eyes and tipping her head. 'You're *going* to have to do that again when you get home.'

Harrison raised his eyebrows, 'Which bit exactly did you like? The part where the girlfriend stabs her lover in the heart?' He smiled and was rewarded by the tinkle of her laugh.

'Yeah it's not nice, but that's just like the *Grimm's Fairy Tales*,' Tanya added. 'They were evil, used to give me nightmares. There was one about a robber bridegroom who was basically a serial killer who was also a cannibal, and even popular ones like "Hansel and Gretel" are about some mad woman in a forest who wanted to eat children and was fattening them up after their father had literally abandoned them in the woods. Who does that?'

Harrison smiled at her earnestness. 'Maybe it was an old-fashioned way of warning children not to trust strangers and wander off in the forest alone.'

'Mmh, not convinced. Anyway, it will be nice to curl up and read a good book together.'

'I'm looking forward to getting back home, too. Jersey is a nice island, but I just feel the longer I'm over here, the colder the trail will get for Desmond Manning.'

'Jack's on the case, I promise you,' Tanya said, her face more serious now. 'We've got a few contingencies in place.'

'I'd rather none of you had anything to do with that man. He's evil. Everyone he goes near, he hurts.'

'Jack is already involved, and I've no intention of going anywhere near Desmond. I'd just like you to stop having to think about him. The sooner we get him put away, the better.'

AFTER HE'D FINISHED his phone call with Tanya, Harrison leaned back on the pillows and sighed. They didn't get to spend much time together because they were always both so busy, but when they did, she always made him feel good. It was a dangerous situation to be in for a man who liked to keep focused.

He read through *The Little Mermaid* one more time, noting down a few things. There were still a lot of options for the motives of the killer, or killers. It could be some kind of cult worshipping a sea sprite, like Mami Wata or Melusine, and yet for him, that didn't quite add up. He was convinced the victim had been prepared carefully right from the start. Maybe he was wrong, and she was a random woman who just happened to have had a lot of bad cosmetic surgery, but he didn't think so. He was getting frustrated. He needed to sleep on it. Tomorrow, he'd go for a run on the beach before going in and see if that could clear his head.

As Harrison drifted off to sleep, he thought about the young woman lying mutilated in the morgue. Surely there must be somebody out there who would have missed her. Someone who knew who she was? Right now, she was literally a nobody who had been transformed into a mermaid and was now famous across the world. Or perhaps that was the key. The mirror in her hand, all the surgery. Perhaps she had craved all this; the attention, the notoriety.

11

Harrison's intention of going for a run first thing in the morning was shattered by a phone call to his mobile at five past seven. He'd just got up and was digging his running gear out of his bag.

'It's happened again.' Harrison could hear the breathless tension in Tracey's voice. 'There's a second mermaid. I'll pick you up in fifteen minutes.'

Tracey didn't wait for him to confirm that he'd be ready. She ended the call.

Harrison abandoned the search for his running kit and instead dived into the bathroom to freshen up, before throwing on his clothes and heading down to reception to ensure he was ready for when Tracey arrived.

She didn't even pull in properly, but stopped in the road, barely putting the brakes on while he got himself into the car and belted up.

'It's the east of the island this time,' she said to him. 'Havre des Pas, just outside of St Helier. Same set up as in St

Ouen. There's a paramedic with her, but the first officer on scene seemed to think it was too late.'

As they turned right towards the sea and came to a mini roundabout, two police officers stood in the road, stopping traffic from driving that way. Tracey pressed the button to wind down her window.

'DI Quenault,' she said to one of the officers, and showed her badge to be waved on through.

They were clearly in a tourist area here, with a big hotel, The Ommaroo, on their left and beach all along the right. A short pier jutted out onto the beach, with a mostly blue and white, curved building at the end. It wasn't a defensive structure like the tower at St Ouen, more of a leisure facility of the type you'd see at the end of the seaside piers in Britain. Despite the fact the sea had retreated a fair way down the beach, a pool of water remained intact alongside the pier end.

'She's on the diving pontoon in the middle of the sea pool,' Tracey said to him, but it was unnecessary. It was easy to see the focus of attention.

The ambulance, police and coastguard vehicles were parked up the road ahead and people had lined the road or were standing on their doorsteps, watching. A group of police officers in fluorescent-yellow jackets stood along the seawall shielding the scene with their bodies as though trying to stop people from seeing. It obviously wasn't working.

Tracey stopped the car in the road and jumped out, not waiting for Harrison.

He got out too and looked across to the pool. From where he stood, he could see her. Lying on her side in the middle of the pool, almost as though she was hovering above the water. Even from here he could tell she had a mirror again – and something white which he couldn't quite make out. He followed Tracey to the edge of the police cordon to ensure he was let through and then hung back while she marched down the slipway onto the beach, so that he could take a good look around.

There were about thirty or forty people lining the road, watching. He heard Tracey bark a command to one of the young PCs. 'Get the Honoraries to clear the road. Park the vehicles up in front here to block them from taking photos.'

She carried on to where Harrison could see Detective Superintendent Graeme Walker talking with a group of officers and paramedics on the beach, at the edge of the pool.

The mermaid was going nowhere, but Harrison wanted to see who was watching, before they got moved on by the police. He stood and looked at the faces along the road, checking every single one. He took his mobile out and pressed record on the video, using it to slowly sweep the whole area. If he missed something now, a face in a window, or a shadow round a corner, he might spot it later on the playback.

A group of building workers were already being moved on, and they sloped off down the road, hands in pockets, lips around cigarettes. A young man and woman disappeared back inside a house. There were several staff from the hotel down the road. They quickly left without further prompting, followed by two older couples who were presumably guests. Directly in front of Harrison was a man parked up in a black Range Rover. It was facing the sea, and he was sat watching impassively. He didn't see Harrison because he was too engrossed in what was going on behind him. Seconds later, one of the police officers walked up to his car and asked him to move on. A short distance away, a cyclist who had been standing staring, got back onto his bike and pedalled in the direction Harrison and Tracey had just come, while two dog walkers stopped their chatting and carried on walking with their bored furry companions.

He scanned the windows of the properties and looked for any other vantage points where somebody could be watching. Finally, when he was sure he'd seen as much as he could, he pocketed his phone and followed Tracey down onto the beach to look at their latest mermaid.

The coastguard had brought a dinghy, which had been used to ferry the paramedic out to the pontoon. That obviously hadn't been available when the first officer had arrived on the scene. The officer was now wrapped in a blanket, dripping from having swum out to the platform to see if he could do anything to help. He'd returned disappointed and soaked for his effort.

DSU Graeme Walker was deep in conversation about logistics and recovery. One of the team had just finished a phone call and was reporting that someone from the States of Jersey was en route to open the sluice gate in order to drain the pool. There was a discussion about erecting some kind of screen in the meantime to prevent any further photography.

Harrison waited until there was a gap in the discussions.

'Detective Superintendent Walker, would it be OK if I go out to her to take a closer look? I'd like to see the scene before it's touched.'

'That's fine, Dr Lane, as long as you don't get out of the boat or come into contact with anything. We can't even begin on forensics until the pool has been emptied.'

Harrison nodded and stepped towards the pool. The water looked quite shallow, but he guessed from the state of the policeman that it got deeper further out. Harrison would have to wade to the boat.

'I'll take you over,' a young man from the coastguard team offered. Harrison nodded his thanks and took his trainers and socks off. He didn't have much in the way of clothes with him, and sitting in wet trainers all day would not be a pleasant experience. Rolling up his jeans, he paddled out a few feet, until the water became deeper and there was enough to ensure the dinghy would take their weight without getting stuck on the sand. The water was cold, a shock to his system seeing as he'd only got out of bed just over half an hour before, but it wasn't as bad as he thought it would be. Clearly, sea temperatures were still that little bit warmer thanks to the heating effect of the summer sun, although they were certainly on the wane.

They rowed over to the platform and, as they got closer, his companion went slowly to ensure no water was sloshed over the victim, who was in the same pose as the first mermaid. In fact, if he hadn't known better, he'd have said she looked almost identical. The same long blonde hair, waspish waist and fish tail. Like her predecessor, she held a mirror in one hand, although it now lay flat, mirror side face down, which was presumably where the officer and paramedic had been trying to find a pulse. Her other hand was clutching several large white feathers. Much bigger than you'd find on a seagull, and pure snowy white. Those were the only objects he could see. Obviously the killer hadn't felt a lamp necessary to attract attention here, and there was definitely no bell.

'She looks like she's just fallen asleep,' the young coastguard almost whispered behind him. 'The paramedic said she could have only been dead around an hour.'

Harrison kept silent. He had nothing to add.

He looked at her face. False eyelashes again, a rich-red lipstick, and enough rouge on her cheeks to take away the pallor of death. Her eyes were closed, and he hoped she hadn't been conscious for long, if at all, after her legs had been amputated. There was no doubting the fact they were gone. The fish tail had been sewn onto her abdomen and curled around her in a way that no legs would have been able to. From what he could tell, she'd undergone the same kinds of cosmetic surgery as the St Ouen mermaid. What chance was there that two girls would have been to the same doctor and had exactly the same procedures?

He looked back to shore, scanning the area for obvious places for someone to sit, wait, and watch. The area reminded him of a Victorian seaside town. He could imagine the promenade along the shoreline bustling with people, and the buildings all around filled with tourists in the days before cheap package holidays to the continent became available. Now with his back to the sea, he looked to the left and saw a big chimney rising up from the headland, and a large grey block of a building. They marred the vista and definitely wouldn't have been around in its heyday. He looked up at the building abutting the pool. It was painted a nautical blue and white, and connected to the promenade by the pier with white seaside railings and lamps all along its length.

A beautiful place, but such a tragic scene.

Why here? What was significant about this place? The murderer ran a greater risk of being seen. There might be CCTV on the buildings, and it was much busier than St Ouen. There had to be a reason for the locations.

Harrison turned his focus back to the mermaid. The concrete platform on which she lay wasn't going to yield any more clues for him; there were no signs to read on its hard, non-porous surface. Forensics would need to come and check every millimetre, but something told Harrison that they were unlikely to find anything. Their killer was clever, clearly planned everything in fine detail to have been able to stage his victims in the locations he'd chosen, and he was forensically aware.

Harrison was convinced, more than ever, that it was a lone killer. There was too much passion put into this for it to be a cult scenario. They worked alone, and almost certainly lived alone. He was also convinced they'd held these young women captive while turning them into the creations they'd become. The question was, did the killer have any more where these two had come from?

12

The sounds of Jennifer screaming and begging The Jailer for mercy had torn all of them into pieces, shredding nerves, and making her hyperventilate. They'd even joined in with the begging and crying at one point. The fear of what was coming to them outdoing any terror they felt by not doing as he told them to do and shutting up.

'I have done everything I promised I would do for you,' he'd said to them. 'Why are you so ungrateful?'

She'd never once seen him raise his voice and shout, not once witnessed him losing his cool, but she saw the veins bulging on his neck and knew that he was angry.

In the end, he'd put his music on. Vivaldi drowned them out until the sound of the electric saw out-screamed them all.

She'd sat in her dark metal prison, her body shivering with fear. It had only been a few days since Maxine had gone. Now Jennifer would be going too. If he carried on choosing them by their arrival time, then it would be Nicky, and then her. She had just days left to live. Just days before her legs would be cut from her and she'd wake up to the stench of fish sewn onto her body.

She retched, bringing up the disgusting pink diet shake she'd been forced to eat earlier. Then she retched again, and again, as outside the saw screeched and ground as it cut through bone. Eventually, when it grew quiet and her stomach and gullet were burnt and bruised with the effort of vomiting, she lay down on her bunk and cried.

In the last year, she'd had plenty of time to think about what had brought her here. The paths she'd chosen in her life that had led to The Jailer. The reality was she'd been a victim long before now. Her story was similar to the others. Unhappy childhoods. Parents who were either absent through choice, in the form of drugs, alcohol or divorce, or because they had died. She remembered Jennifer crying the day she'd told them all about her mother's cancer diagnosis and the subsequent heart attack that had taken her father when he heard the news. Two months of nursing her dying mother and she'd been left alone in the world. Just turned fourteen and thrust into a care system that barely registered her existence, let alone her grief.

Her own story had started differently. She remembered happy times as a young child, but then her father walked out on them, preferring his office secretary who was fifteen years her mother's junior. He'd never looked back, starting a new family all over again, and her mother had turned to the bottle and any man she could find who made her feel attractive and wanted. Her selfish needs left no love for her daughter and that fed into her weight issues and the bullying at school. Misery fed on misery. That had been all of their unifying similarities. They'd all been loners with no support and no vision for a future. Hope, a fairy tale, and the promise that everyone would know their names and call them beautiful, had been the lure. It had been an easy sell.

She looked at her body. It didn't feel like hers and though the scars from the surgery might be small, they felt like massive white gashes on her skin. She looked now like she'd only ever dreamed she could look. He'd made her perfect, just as he'd promised, but this perfect body would never be loved by another person, wear a wedding ring on her finger, or give birth to a baby she could love and nurture, giving it everything her mother had failed to offer. She wouldn't walk barefoot on a beach, or wear high heels again. She would go down in history, but still as the victim she'd always been.

She wondered what the headlines would really say about them. Would the papers print photos of her as a schoolgirl, and drag out her old headmistress, who would say what a charming girl she had been, liked by everyone. Such a waste. That's what they always said, wasn't it? Even though they might not mean it. No one talks badly of the dead. She doubted her old headmistress would even remember who she was.

She guessed they might hunt her mother down, too. Find her pickled in some English bar in Spain, eating fish and chips with her thug of a boyfriend. He might have stopped hitting her by now, but she doubted it. Leopards don't change their spots. She could see her mother plastering on the make-up and feigning the tears for her darling daughter, taken from her by this brutal killer. She'd be able to get drinks on the back of that story for months. The mother of a mermaid. It would be the biggest achievement of her mother's life.

As the months of captivity had worn on, she'd contemplated self-harming, ruining his beautiful creation, but one of the others had tried that and he'd tied her hands and made her wear some kind of straitjacket suit like she'd seen asylum patients wearing in horror movies. Perhaps if she did it just before it was her turn, then he would have to wait for the damage to heal – but what would be the point of that? It would merely prolong her torturous existence and end one of the others' earlier instead. She wanted release now. She wanted to escape this hell pit, and if the only way was to have her legs taken and die, then she was ready to embrace it.

13

With nothing further for Harrison and Tracey to do at the beach, they both returned to the station. By the time they'd left, an entire squad of emergency services personnel were being forced to hold up privacy sheeting to shield their victim from the gathering media who had wormed their way through police cordons. Their biggest fear was a drone going up, and so they were working feverishly to get the pool drained and a forensic tent over mermaid number two.

As they walked back to Tracey's car, Digby had shouted across to them from the media line. 'A second mermaid, do you have a serial killer on your hands, DI Quenault?'

'Morning, Digby. I'm sorry, you know the score, I'm not going to comment on or off record.'

He wasn't going to give up either; he carried on throwing his questions across the road at her. 'I've heard it's a mysterious mermaid cult based in France. Are you talking to French police or Interpol?'

Tracey carried on ignoring him.

Digby wouldn't give up. 'I understand they hack the girls' legs off to give them their tails. It's not quite the fairy story it seems, is it, DI Quenault?'

Tracey had her hand on the car door handle, but stopped and turned round to him. 'As I said. I'm unable to comment on or off record, but I'm sure we'll be arranging a press conference later today and you'll be able to ask your questions then.' She slumped into the car with a big sigh.

Harrison thought she'd handled it all very calmly. He wouldn't have even bothered answering the toe rag.

'Knew it was only a matter of time before it got out about the legs,' she had said to Harrison as they headed back to the station. 'That should put off a few of the Disney *Little Mermaid* fans.'

THE MOOD back at the station was sombre and frustrated. They'd made absolutely no headway with their first victim, and now they had a second. The killer was operating right under their noses and they still had no idea of his identity, or even who the victims were.

The incident room was conspicuously absent of Detective Superintendent Walker.

'There's a development at the harbour,' Tracey told Harrison. 'A French boat. He went straight down there.'

Harrison had just logged onto the computer system when DSU Walker and a couple of other officers arrived back in the room.

'OK, your attention, quickly!' he barked at the team. Harrison could see he was wired. They'd clearly made some kind of headway and he wasted no time in sharing the news with the team.

'We've just detained three French nationals at the harbour. We got a tip-off about them and they match the description of the men seen at St Ouen. They arrived the afternoon after the first Mermaid was found there. They could easily have been out at sea before coming into port. We've got Harbours checking on their movements now. They're fishermen, and yet they're not out at sea. I find that strange. When we went on board, there was a statue of a mermaid in the wheelhouse. Are they part of some French mermaid cult? Or completely unconnected? We need to find out what they're doing here or at the very least eliminate them from our inquiry.'

He scanned the room and spotted Tracey and Harrison.

'Tracey, could you and Dr Lane talk to them and assess if they're involved? Mark can go in with you, he's fluent in French.'

'Sir,' Tracey replied, tipping a nod to DS Mark Le Scelleur, who was sitting across from her.

'I don't need to tell you all that we now have a second victim,' the detective superintendent continued. 'Forensics and recovery are underway, but the MO looks to be identical to our first victim. She has been posed the same, been sewn into her fishtail in the same way, and was also holding a mirror, along with what looks to be swan's feathers. We assume nothing. The men in the interview rooms may be totally unconnected to this case, so until we have positive confirmation they are, we keep looking for our killer. I want a wrap up meeting this afternoon to assess where we're at. Now get to it.'

At the mention of the word *swan*, Harrison's mind remembered something he'd read last night. His jigsaw pieces were starting to come together.

'We'd better go,' Tracey said. 'They've not been officially

arrested, so are here voluntarily to help with the inquiry. I don't want to give them an excuse to disappear off.'

THE MEN WERE in interview rooms on the ground floor. As with any police interview situation, they'd been separated to avoid any further collaboration in their stories. DI Tracey Quenault, DS Mark Le Scelleur and Harrison went into the reception area to get the details.

'You've got a Marcel Lepretre in room one, Olivier Beaun in two, and Jean Dupont in three,' the receptionist told Tracey.

'Thanks, Maggie,' she replied.

'Let's start in room one then,' she said to her two colleagues, and after touching her security pass to the panel, she let them back into the secure area of the building and through the first door on her right.

The room had plain painted walls with plastic chairs and a table, all fixed. There was no security bar around the wall like there was in the custody suites. It was felt the panic alarm strip which ran the length of the room in case things turned ugly wasn't necessary here. Victims and eyewitnesses were interviewed, rather than suspects and those who'd been arrested.

Marcel Lepretre was sat facing them, slouched over the table. He looked up as they entered.

'Bonjour, Monsieur Lepretre.'

He nodded in response.

'Peut on parler anglais?' Tracey continued in clumsy French.

Another nod.

'Thank you, Mr Lepretré. I'm afraid my French is limited. I'm Detective Inspector Tracey Quenault, and this is

Detective Sergeant Mark Le Scelleur, and Dr Harrison Lane.'

Marcel Lepretre was a well-built man in his late thirties, clearly used to being outdoors and not sat in a plastic-filled enclosed space. There was a slight odour of fish in the room, a hazard of his occupation. Despite the fact they were inside, he'd kept his beanie hat on.

Marcel eyed Harrison, who had gone to stand in the corner, leaving the two chairs facing him for the detectives. The man's eyes were pink-rimmed and bloodshot. Something in his demeanour made Harrison think the reason why had more to do with an emotional issue than a little too much of the duty-free spirits.

'Thank you for agreeing to come in today and talk to us.' Tracey pulled Marcel's focus back to her. She sat down opposite him, and Mark took the chair next to her.

'As you know, we are investigating a double murder in the island. Two young women who have been mutilated to look like mermaids, and left to die.'

'Two?' Marcel looked surprised.

'Yes, we found a second victim this morning.'

Harrison was watching Marcel's face closely. The surprise was genuine. It had shocked him into being more attentive.

'We understand that yourself and your two colleagues were seen yesterday at St Ouen, where the first victim was found. Do you want to tell us about that?'

Marcel nodded. 'My brother, Sebastian. We lost him off board two week ago in bad seas. This was our first trip since.' Marcel hung his head and hesitated. 'I struggle with it. Olivier suggest we come to St Helier for a day or two so I can pull my head straight.'

Marcel's English was better than both Harrison and Tracey's French, but it wasn't perfect.

'Why St Helier and not your home port?' Tracey questioned.

'A change. At home we talk nothing but Sebastian.' He looked up at her. Harrison guessed that his culture and way of life gave little room for male emotions. The pain was etched on his face, in the way he sat, and even in his voice. Marcel was a man struggling with his mental health after bereavement.

'How did Sebastian die?' Tracey asked him gently.

'Taken monstre wave. He was not so experienced. It was me who ask him to come. Usually it is three, but we knew bad weather was coming. We think four would get the work done faster.'

'Can I ask why you went to St Ouen?'

'Me and Sebastian, we lived in Dominica as children. We watch the Mami Wata festival there and he always remember it. Now Sebastian, he is artist and make mermaid sculptures.'

'Mami Wata, this is the African and Afro-Caribbean water spirit you talked about yesterday?' Tracey turned and addressed Harrison now, who nodded in reply.

'Are there others who believe in Mami Wata back home?' Tracey returned her focus to Marcel.

He frowned and shook his head; it was clear he didn't understand her question.

'You said Sebastian believed in Mami Wata, did others?'

He frowned again. 'No. Sebastian did not believe like the Dominicans.' Marcel shifted uncomfortably and took his time to continue. 'I do not know why I take things. It... it just was right for me.'

Harrison saw nothing but depression in his body language. He was telling the truth and clearly struggling not only with the grief but also guilt. He didn't fit the profile physically either. His hands were large and rough, definitely not the kind of hands that could perform intricate surgery.

They got very little more out of Marcel, so Tracey thanked him and all three went to stand outside in the corridor before moving on to room two.

'I don't get why he thought to go and do that. What makes a grown man leave an offering for a mermaid?' Tracey said to Harrison.

'It's what makes us human. It's why we touch wood, or wave at magpies, why we hate it when we smash a mirror or are happy if a black cat crosses our path. We search for hope in everything, even death. Ultimately, it's why we believe in religion, the ultimate hope of an eternal life and a fatherly figure looking out for us.

'He connected with the mermaid because to him, it was a sign that his brother hadn't gone. I see it so often in the bereaved; when a loved one goes, the person left behind starts seeing a bird, insect or animal, something that the one who is gone had particularly connected with in life. We search for evidence of a message from beyond the grave, of hope, in all manner of ways.'

Tracey didn't have a reply to Harrison's logic and the truth of it showed on her face. Instead, she took a deep breath and sighed, before heading into the second interview room.

'Bonjour, Monsieur Beaun, parlez-vous anglais?' Tracey said to Olivier Beaun as she entered room two and held out her hand in greeting.

The man shook his head but met Tracey's hand. He was blonde with the same outdoor look as Marcel.

'OK, Mark, you're going to have to take over. I've just exhausted all my schoolgirl French.' Tracey smiled at her colleague.

Harrison was only able to understand around half of the

conversation, but it was clear that it went along the same lines as Marcel's story. They could have collaborated and agreed on what line they were going to spin the police, but he didn't think so. When DS Mark Le Scelleur wrapped up the interview, they went back to the corridor for a quick chat before continuing.

'He didn't add anything that Marcel hadn't already told us,' the DS said to Tracey.

'Yeah, I'm not looking forward to telling Graeme that his prime suspects don't seem to be connected in any way, but I think that's exactly what we're going to have to do. What do you think, Harrison?'

'I believe neither man so far fits the profile.'

'Profile? So you've come up with one?'

'I believe I'm close. But even looking at their hands, you can see that they're not made for the kind of surgery and needlework that our killer has been doing.'

'*If* the killer has been doing it.'

'You saw the second victim. She's virtually identical. What chance is there that the killer would have found two girls who'd had the same procedures in the same way and ended up looking the same? He's creating them himself.'

'Or *they* are,' Tracey added.

Harrison didn't respond. He wasn't sure if she was being purposefully challenging in a devil's advocate kind of way to stimulate thought, or because she was determined that they still looked for a cult.

'OK, Mark, we're due at Dr Chaudhry's to speak to the plastic surgeon from the UK. Do you think you can handle the third guy for us on your own?' she asked.

'Yeah, course,' DS Le Scelleur replied.

'Then we'll have to cut them loose, but make sure you let Graeme know and double-check with him first.'

'Oh great, make me the sacrificial messenger,' Mark replied, only half joking.

'Tell him I'll fill him in at the briefing later,' Tracey said, already on her way out through the door.

Harrison followed in her wake as she headed to her car.

'We can grab a coffee and bite to eat on the way back,' Tracey said to him. 'I'm presuming you're not wanting anything before we visit the mermaids?'

'That's fine,' Harrison replied, already not looking forward to the upcoming attack on his nostrils.

'So you've come up with a profile then?' Tracey probed. 'Care to give me the highlights?'

'I want to speak with the plastic surgeon first, but I'm absolutely convinced we're dealing with just one man, not a cult or group.'

Tracey raised her eyebrows and pulled a face. 'How can you be so sure?'

'I'll explain later,' Harrison replied.

She didn't look too pleased with that response, but he wasn't ready to share his thoughts yet, not until he'd spoken to the cosmetic surgeon, who he was convinced would back up his theory that they were dealing with a highly organised and intelligent psychopath.

14

They found Guy Kloss bent over the remains of the first mermaid, studying the scar tissue on her abdomen. He looked up at their arrival, intelligent blue eyes showing through the surgical mask, hair protector and full suit.

'DI Quenault and Dr Lane,' Dr Chaudhry said as though they were being announced at a wedding or banquet.

Harrison had forgotten just how much he hated the smell of fish and death mingled together, but it didn't seem to perturb Dr Chaudhry or Mr Kloss.

'Mr Guy Kloss, consultant surgeon in plastic surgery,' Chaudhry continued with his announcements.

'Good afternoon,' Guy said and his eyes smiled at them politely.

'Thank you for coming over to consult,' Tracey took charge. 'Have you been briefed on the case?'

'As much as I need to be, yes thank you.'

'We need to know if you can tell where she might have

undergone her surgery and any other information about who, what, why and when.'

He nodded.

'Dr Chaudhry, has the second victim been brought in yet?'

'She has recently arrived. My team are prepping and I'm going to start the examination shortly.'

'OK, then perhaps Mr Kloss could also take a look over her?'

'Yes, of course,' both men replied.

'In answer to your question, where did she get her surgery? That I couldn't tell you,' Guy began. 'What I can say is that this isn't to the professional standards of the UK, so they're not procedures which would have been carried out legally there. However, from some of the techniques used, I think the surgeon, if we can call him that, had both medical training and some very basic plastic surgery training. The principles are there, but these techniques were used some time ago. We've improved our understanding and methods considerably since. Add to this the less than professional way in which they have been carried out, and I'd say this person underwent their training probably around two decades or so ago, and hasn't been practising. Until now.'

'You can tell it's just one person? Or could it be more?' Tracey pressed.

'Yes, looks like all the same handiwork.'

'Could they be a practising doctor but just not a plastic surgeon?'

'It's possible. Surgical skill sets are considerably different to being a GP, for example.'

'We think the victim was originally overweight, is that your opinion also?'

'Yes, absolutely. You can see where the skin has been

stretched, and the operation to remove ribs would have had the effect of making her look slimmer.'

Harrison had listened up to this point, but spoke now.

'Would she have been able to carry on a normal life while undergoing these operations, during and after?'

'Interesting question. She's had a lot of work done, and over a fairly short period of time. We wouldn't recommend doing as much as this all so fast. Ignoring the fact we've already ascertained our surgeon doesn't follow professional standards, I think she would have struggled to lead a normal life. The recovery times alone would have been an issue. If she was working and socialising, then it would have been noticeable for sure.

'The ribs, for example: he's taken out not just the eleventh and twelfth, but also the tenth. Rib surgery now would be achieved in as non-invasive a way as possible, but he's cut her quite substantially to get at the area he wanted to inside. He's no keyhole surgeon, that's for sure. The tenth rib runs not just around the front, but also back and front. It's a tougher removal process. Plus, he's also undertaken a breast reduction. She'd have had a rough few months coping with all this so-called surgery. It's more like skilled butchery to me.'

'Could he have just learnt all this on the internet?' Tracey asked.

'Highly unlikely. He's definitely had practice before with suture work. This level of surgery is old school, and he's out of practice, but there's some knowledge there.'

'Would a nurse who assists surgeons be able to do this?'

'It's possible, but again, the issue with that is that these aren't modern techniques. If they were a nurse or surgical assistant, then you'd expect to see more modern methods being used.'

'Could that be because they don't have the equipment? I

mean keyhole surgery to me sounds like you need some quite sophisticated gadgets,' she continued.

'Keyhole surgery, yes, but it's more subtle than that. He's made cuts in places that nowadays we'd know are not going to yield the best results. It's also a bit slash and burn rather than enhance and improve. He's cut and taken away mostly, like a sculptor. There's a clear sense of what he is trying to achieve, and he's just chipped away and got rid of what he doesn't want.'

'Is there any way to tell if the same man who carried out the cosmetic work also took her legs?' Harrison asked now.

'Well, I assumed it was; let me take another look to be sure.' Guy moved to halfway down the examination table and took a moment to study the mermaid. 'So, it's quite interesting what he's done here,' Guy said, looking up at them. 'He removed the legs and then carried out some remedial work to prevent her from dying immediately from blood loss due to the arteries being severed. However, there was blood loss, and that's because he stopped short of completely stemming the flow. The suturing looks to be the same hand. So yes, I'd say the same man, or woman, did it all.'

'Why would you do that? If he wanted to kill her, why didn't he just let her bleed out and be done with it?' Tracey was addressing Harrison more than the doctors. She still couldn't quite buy into the idea that their perpetrator had been holding the women and operating on them for months.

'He was creating perfection in his eyes,' Harrison replied. 'What he didn't want was for her to be ruined by death. If he'd let her die before she was found, blood would have pooled and decomposition would have started. He couldn't let her bleed out totally because then rigor mortis would also have set in. He placed her at St Ouen at least two hours before she was found. He knew she wouldn't survive, but he wanted her to be as beautiful as possible for that moment. Finally, the mirror gives a clue too. He left her a mirror to see herself. She probably wasn't conscious long, but he wanted her to see herself as we found her.'

Tracey shook her head. Not because she didn't believe Harrison, but at the mentality of the man who'd done this.

'Can we view the second mermaid quickly?' Harrison asked Dr Chaudhry. 'I'd like to see her close up before the examination, while she's still intact – and it would be good to get Mr Kloss's opinion to ensure we are dealing with the same killer, and surgeon, on both.'

'Of course, of course, no problem,' Dr Chaudhry said and directed them out of the room and into another, where the woman found that morning was now lying on a metal examination table.

Both doctors had taken their gloves off and now replaced them with a clean pair. It was critical that no cross-contamination took place between the two bodies.

Tracey hung back. Harrison couldn't blame her. The second victim still wore her fish tail because the post-mortem examination hadn't yet started and it was both shocking and incongruous to see her lying there intact, a real mermaid – of sorts. Harrison had already seen her up close on the rock, the image indelibly scarred into his mind. He stepped forward with the doctors.

Her face showed make-up had been carefully applied. False eyelashes and some kind of cream foundation which covered any blemishes on her skin. Her eyes were virtually shut, but there was no missing the bright-blue colour, exactly like the first victim. He could also see the edge of the contact lenses; it was another lie. Blue wasn't her natural eye colour. Likewise, her hair was blonde and, again, just like the first victim's, it had been dyed.

'She looks remarkably like the other girl!' Guy exclaimed first, voicing the same thought everyone in the room had already had. 'Remarkable.'

He bent over her and carefully examined the scars and blemishes on her body, helped by Dr Chaudhry.

'OK, so rapid weight loss is apparent again,' he said to them, looking intently at her skin, particularly around her midriff. 'Looks like the ribs have been taken out. All the same procedures and I'm pretty sure from the suture scars that we're looking at the same surgeon.' He looked up at Tracey. 'You've got one crazy serial killer on your hands.'

15

DI Tracey Quenault was silent on their way back to the station. Harrison could detect her sombre mood, unsurprising given what they'd both just viewed and heard. A heavy blanket of sadness enveloped the car. Apart from a quick stop off for a sandwich in a local mini supermarket, neither of them said a word until they got back to the station. Harrison felt the weight on his shoulders and he carried it into the incident room with him.

When they arrived back, Tracey checked in with DS Mark Le Scelleur first, to see how he'd got on with the last French fisherman.

'Nothing new. None of them have any links that I can see. They've got alibis for most of their time here and the story about the brother of Marcel checks out. I can't see that we could charge them for anything other than littering the beach.'

'Yeah, I agree. I presume Graeme did too?'

Mark didn't have the opportunity to reply because Detective Superintendent Graeme Walker had spotted Tracey from across the incident room.

'DI Quenault! Are you ready for a quick team update? The lab has just got back with DNA results.'

'Yes, sir,' she replied.

The hubbub in the room slowly settled as officers finished phone calls and joined their colleagues in focusing their attention to the front where Walker had the smart board ready. As soon as they were all gathered, he began.

'First off, Tracey, what of the three fishermen that we brought in earlier?'

'OK, we can eliminate them from the inquiry. They put into St Helier harbour because one of them is having some mental health issues following the death of his brother at sea a couple of weeks ago. Mark's checked out their alibis and they stick.'

'What were they doing at St Ouen then?' Walker addressed Harrison. 'You agree they're unconnected, Dr Lane?'

'I do. It's as Tracey said, he's a man struggling with grief and guilt. The offerings were to a spiritual deity that he and his brother used to see being celebrated in Dominica, where they grew up. Mami Wata is a mermaid-like figure from Africa who travelled to the Caribbean islands with the slaves who were taken from there. It was a sentimental gesture prompted by the discovery of the mermaid victim and his grief.'

'And nothing further from French authorities, either,' DS Le Scelleur added. 'No sign of a cult operating there or in Europe, that could relate to our inquiry.'

'OK, well the good news is we have made some headway with identifying our victim,' DSU Walker revealed. 'The DNA and isotope analysis says that she is British, probably most likely Northern England. DS Prentice, I believe you have someone from the lab on the line now so that we can get this explained?'

'Yes, sir, putting it through now.'

There was a brief pause, and then the sound of distant talking came out of the speakers. 'Arthur Wayne is on the line from Sinclair Forensic lab in Hertfordshire.'

'Good afternoon, Mr Wayne, this is Detective Superintendent Graeme Walker in Jersey. Thank you for taking the time to explain these results to the team.'

'It's not a problem, Detective Superintendent.'

'Can I ask you firstly then to explain how reliable this data is. Are we definitely looking at the identity of a woman from Northern England?'

'Of course, let me explain. Her DNA will show you where other family members, through time, have originated. So, in your victim's case, she has 73% England and Northwest, 16% Welsh, 6% Scottish, 3% Irish and 2% Swedish. We have all been impacted by the migration and invasions of other nations, and so the Swedish, for example, is likely to be Viking blood. A 73% rate for England and the Northwest shows you that a large percentage of her family line has been from that area.'

There was a pause and the sound of computer keys and a mouse being clicked. 'The isotope investigation looks at the atoms effectively within every living thing, and studies the ratios of different chemical elements within them. I won't bore you with the science, but it basically is able to reconstruct the environment that person experienced while they were alive. Diet, nutritional stress, places of residence can all be determined. The teeth will tell us the childhood influences, because they're formed in early childhood, and the bones will give us the adult experiences.

'The isotope analysis of your victim confirms the DNA profile result: that she was brought up and spent most of her life in the north of England. The strontium analysis also ties in with a geological profile around the North-west region. This isn't conclusive in itself, but all the results, including the meteorological profile from the isotopic composition of oxygen, all indicate the same area. I'd therefore say that this result is very reliable.'

'Thank you, that's useful. And are you able to tell if she's been anywhere else in the last year or so?'

'There isn't unfortunately sufficient data to be able to determine where she was in the last year, but her nails and hair showed us that she did undergo a period of dietary stress. In other words, some kind of starvation or extreme diet.'

The whole room seemed to give a collective 'mmmh' when Arthur Wayne had finished.

'Thank you, Mr Wayne, your input is very much appreciated.'

The detective superintendent turned to look at the board for a moment, processing what they'd just heard.

'Right, that's a breakthrough for us because we now have an area in England that we can concentrate on in terms of trying to find somebody who knew our victim before she turned up as a mermaid. Was she kidnapped? We still don't know if she was here or on the continent prior to her death, or even in the UK. That's less likely due to the distance needed to transport the victims, but if we can find out who she was, then we could get the answer to where she has been. Somebody must recognise her and have known her.'

He scanned the faces in front of him, ensuring the team was fully concentrating. 'Tracey, I believe you've just come from seeing Dr Chaudhry. Anything from our second victim yet?'

'Nothing yet, sir, he hadn't started the autopsy, but we did get some interesting information from Guy Kloss, the plastic surgeon who is over from the UK.'

'Ah yes, what did he say?'

'He confirmed Dr Lane's theory that the killer is the one who is carrying out the surgical procedures on the girls.'

'So that makes it more likely that they were held here because the killer wouldn't have had time to transport them once their tails are on. Even France would be pushing it. Did Mr Kloss mention if it was definitely just one person?'

'He did – and confirmed it was the same person for both girls.'

'So that narrows down the field considerably then, surely. We need to find a man who is either a practising or retired plastic surgeon,' DSU Walker said hopefully.

'Possibly,' Tracey replied hesitantly. 'While Mr Kloss said the perpetrator had medical knowledge and received some training in cosmetic surgery, it was at least two decades ago. The techniques used were consistent with old ways of doing things, not modern standards. He also wasn't a fully trained cosmetic surgeon by the looks of it, which fits with what Dr Chaudhry said.'

'So, Doctor Lane, your hunch was correct. It's looking likely that we're dealing with kidnap and imprisonment as well as murder. Do you have any other insights yet?'

'Yes. With two victims, we know a lot more about our killer now,' Harrison said, standing up. He found it easier to talk to a room when he was standing rather than sitting. He wasn't so keen on the detective superintendent saying it had been a hunch, but he let that pass.

'I definitely don't think we're dealing with a cult. It is one man with psychopathic tendencies. He's very intelligent and high functioning. Quite possibly a successful businessman. This is deeply personal to him. He has chosen these women and then turned them into his idea of a perfect mermaid. They're almost identical in looks, so he has a clear pattern for what he is trying to achieve, or whom he is trying to make them look like. Why? I'm not entirely sure yet. He will have groomed them carefully, possibly online, looking for women who won't be missed. That way he runs no risk of there being a big missing person investigation that could potentially track the movements of his victims.'

Harrison took a swig of water, and then continued. 'I have a strong suspicion he is following the original "The Little Mermaid" story by Hans Christian Andersen. Don't confuse it with the Disney version. It starts with six mermaid sisters and one by one they are allowed to go to the surface when they reach the age of fifteen. The first sister heard the pealing of church bells and thought they were wonderful. The second sister saw a flock of swans. That, you'll appreciate, ties in with the bell and swan feathers that were found with the first two victims.'

The room had gone totally silent now, listening to Harrison.

'I think the mirror is to show them how beautiful they are. He is incredibly proud of his own work. You can see that in the meticulous way that he stages them. He keeps them alive until the last possible moment, so that they're the most beautiful they can be when found. He doesn't want death ruining the effect. He has kept those girls locked up some-where and slowly turned them into what we see today.'

'Why?' the detective superintendent asked the question on everyone's lips.

'I'm not quite clear on the motivation yet, but it is something deeply personal. It could be related to his own child-hood, or possibly to his own child or partner. Something will have triggered this, maybe a death or divorce, or potentially a job loss. It won't be because he's emotionally upset about what happened. He doesn't love or feel in the way that we do. It will be because control has been taken out of his hands, or that something or somebody he feels responsible for has been taken away or left him.

'It's very possible he lives alone because creating these girls has taken a long time. He's not going to be the kind of man who sits with his feet up watching TV. He's driven. Ruth-less. In his head he has a clear purpose: to regain control of that trigger situation. He might even believe he's doing these women a favour by turning them into something beautiful.'

'How do we catch him?'

'With difficulty. His intelligence, and most likely good social standing, will keep him hidden. He's going to have money. All this preparation takes cash. However, this man is an egotist. He wants the world to be talking about his creations. He might well end up coming to us, desperate to get close to the investigation, his investigation. That will be his Achilles heel. While we wait for him, we need to work backwards. I suspect he found these girls on some internet forum. If we can work out their identities, then we might be able to figure out how he got in contact with them and follow the trail that way.'

'Thank you, Dr Lane,' Walker said.

'There's something else. Something we must all keep in mind,' Harrison added. 'In the Hans Christian Andersen story, there were six mermaid sisters. I don't think we've heard the last from him. I fear that he may have up to four more girls locked up somewhere, ready to turn into mermaids and fulfil his purpose.'

16

The briefing left the team with mixed feelings. On the one hand, they finally felt like they had some information on the killer and victims that they could work with, but on the other, Harrison's warning that there could be four more girls about to die had been a depressing one.

Harrison was convinced that the killer would have been at the scene when the mermaids were discovered, and so he downloaded the video he'd taken on his phone at Havre des Pas and started looking through it again, scanning every detail to see if he could spot anything or anyone who looked like they might fit the profile.

Tracey walked back over to her desk, slapped her note-book down onto its surface, and asked, 'You really think there's four more of them out there?'

'I think there is a strong possibility.'

She rubbed the back of her neck and sighed.

'We're focusing on how the killer has been transporting them and upping our presence at the ports. We're thinking boat is the likeliest route; it's easier to get stuff in than the airport because you could land at an out-of-the-way bay at night if needs be. Besides, we know he's comfortable in a boat because there was no other way he could have put victim one on that rock in St Ouen. CCTV shows that there wasn't anybody on the beach that night; he had to come in via sea.

'DC Peter Edwards is with Customs, seeing who has brought in medical supplies or equipment over the last few years, but I'm not holding out much hope that our killer's done that through the proper channels. Plus, we're getting a list together of every practising and retired doctor and surgeon on the island. There can't be that many of them in a population of just over a hundred thousand. We'll find him,' she said, looking determinedly at Harrison. 'We're also going to hold a press conference in about an hour. Try to get the media on side to help us find these two girls. Mr Kloss has advised on a new e-fit of what they'd have looked like prior to their surgery. Want to see?' Tracey pulled up a couple of images onto her computer screen.

Harrison stood up and went to stand behind her.

'This is the St Ouen mermaid. She looks so different, doesn't she?' Tracey said sadly. On her screen was a front on and profile view e-fit of a young woman with light brown hair. She was overweight, but her face was kind and human, unlike the perfect, sculptured half-fish that she had become. 'I just can't believe someone would go to all this trouble. It must have taken him ages.'

'He's driven, totally focused. It's why he will have also been successful in business. That and the fact he won't have cared about anyone's feelings like you or I would.'

'Would you take part in the press conference with me?' Tracey turned and looked up at him.

'No. I don't do media. The last thing I want is to be

distracted by journalists.' Harrison shook his head. 'I will come and watch, though. He might go along.'

'You think? Is there anything we can say that might draw him out?'

Harrison thought for a few moments. 'Not that I'd recommend at this stage. Once we have an idea of who he might be, there are some definite triggers which could give us confirmation, but I wouldn't want to use those yet.'

THE MEDIA BRIEFING was being held in The Royal Yacht hotel's conference room, which was just across the road from Harrison's hotel. Harrison made his own way there half an hour later than Tracey and DSU Walker, keen to avoid arriving early and being conspicuous.

The Royal Yacht overlooked Weighbridge Place, an open event space with two sides framed by bars, restaurants and the hotel, one side running by the main road into the tunnel, and shelters and a taxi rank – which Harrison imagined would be particularly busy on Friday and Saturday nights – along the final side. Even in the chill conditions of early December, The Royal Yacht's outdoor seating area was busy with people looking cosy and warm at tables thanks to the glowing orange parasol heaters and glass panelling which protected the alfresco area from the wind coming off the sea.

He walked into the hotel entrance and saw a sign directing him up to the first floor for the media briefing. Ahead of him, a camera crew was lugging their equipment up the stairs. They rushed into the room, clearly fretting that they were late because it was already packed with photographers, their cameras, and reporters. Harrison wondered if there was any news going on anywhere else in the world, because it seemed like the news crews were all here in Jersey.

It was the perfect story for them: murder, mystery, a beautiful fairy tale creature. It had everything a journalist could hope for.

Harrison slipped in right at the back, trying to melt into the corner of the room unseen. At the front, he could see Digby, clearly in his element with his pack and behaving like a playful silverback gorilla. The man had obviously decided he'd reached the pinnacle of his career and was enjoying it.

Tracey and Detective Superintendent Graeme Walker filed in from a side door, both of them looking serious and professional. She didn't look at the audience and Harrison detected nerves in her body language; her walk was stiff and self-conscious. He wasn't surprised that she felt this way. Most people would be anxious ahead of a briefing like this. Reporters could ask awkward questions, and then there was the prospect of cameras and microphones being shoved into your face and getting tongue tied. He hadn't said no to doing it with her for that reason. Harrison was used to giving his professional opinion and if he wasn't sure of something, then he'd say, but he liked to stay in the background, away from public view. He only wanted to answer to the senior investigating officer he was working with, and the victims.

'Thank you all for coming.' The detective superintendent smiled at the room. 'I'm Detective Superintendent Graeme Walker, and sitting next to me is Detective Inspector Tracey Quenault, who is senior investigating officer on this case. As you all know, a second victim was found this morning at Harve des Pas. The circumstances and the mode of death appear to be identical to the St Ouen killing.' Harrison noticed that the DSU had purposely not referred to them as mermaids. He was trying to keep the story to facts and reality, and make the assembled media realise they were dealing with a cold-hearted murderer, not somebody who was creating miracles to make little girls smile.

Harrison switched off to what he was saying and pulled his focus away from the two police officers. He wasn't here to listen to information he already knew; he was here to look at the audience in the hope that their killer might have come to bask in the glory of his work.

Harrison started systematically scanning around the room, studying every face and looking for the cuckoo in the nest. He had a good idea of the type of man he would be looking for, but, even for Harrison, it was hard to determine potential suspects just from looking at the back of their heads.

By the time DSU Walker had finished his set statement, and Tracey was showing the e-fits and asking the reporters in the room to publish them, Harrison had managed to discount a good percentage of the room and boiled his list of men he wanted to investigate further down to seven. Questions were starting and Digby was first to fling his arm into the air.

'Can you confirm that the women died from blood loss after having their legs amputated?' Digby asked.

Tracey threw a glance at DSU Walker.

'Yes, that's correct. The killer amputated their legs in order to be able to make their lower bodies fit into a fish's tail. We are dealing with a dangerous and callous man.'

'Was it a real fish tail?' Digby pushed.

'It was,' Tracey replied. She quickly moved her eyes away from him and to the other side of the room. 'The woman in the blue suit,' she said.

'Thank you. Elize Robertson, BBC. It was suggested that some kind of cult was behind these murders. Is that still your line of inquiry?'

Tracey threw a look at the back of the room where

Harrison stood. 'No. We believe that one man is behind this, but I can't give you any more details than that as obviously this is a live and fast-moving inquiry.'

Harrison spotted one of his seven potential suspects turn and make a comment to somebody sitting alongside him. They both sniggered. It was enough for Harrison to be able to discount him. Now he had six.

The questions continued for another ten minutes before DSU Walker called an end to the briefing. By the time he did, Harrison only had three left, and he wasn't too hopeful about them. As the room erupted and everyone stood up, some made a dash for the exit to file stories, and others surged forward to ask Tracey and the superintendent for an interview.

He watched his last three prospects closely. One guy, dressed in a neat suit, looked the part, but as he made his way through the throng, Harrison could tell there wasn't a confident bone in his body. Harrison was looking for an egotistical psychopath, and this young man definitely didn't fit the bill.

Two left. These two were slightly older, which was more like what he'd expect. One of them walked towards the back of the room, his demeanour serious. As he got closer to Harrison, his face lit up, and he put his hand out and smiled broadly at a cameraperson. He was an American reporter. That left just one man.

Harrison's last potential suspect was heading straight for the exit door. But Harrison wasn't going to let him walk away without checking him out. As the man walked past, Harrison pushed himself off the wall that he'd been leaning on and followed him out.

He spotted a thin company brochure lying on a table and grabbed it, taking his opportunity while he could. 'Excuse me, excuse me,' he repeated as he caught up with the man and almost stepped in front of him to stop him. 'Sorry, I believe you dropped this,' he added, holding out the brochure.

The man looked at Harrison, then at the brochure, and shook his head. 'Nothing to do with me, mate,' he replied and went to turn away.

'You a reporter?' Harrison asked him.

Another shake of the head and what could only be described as a grimace. 'No. Police. Detective Constable Phillip Breton.' The man raised his eyebrows. Harrison could tell he was expecting him to react.

'OK, no problem. Sorry to have bothered you,' Harrison replied.

He stood still, as though looking on his phone, but took a photograph of DC Breton as he turned to walk down the stairs, just in case. Wouldn't be the first time that a criminal had impersonated a police officer, but if he was honest, he didn't think this was his man. The killer hadn't come to the press conference after all.

17

Harrison was disappointed, but he wasn't beaten. It was just a matter of time before the killer showed his hand. He was sure of it. In the meantime, he'd keep on looking.

He was about to head back to the station when a text came through on his phone.

> Can you do a quick Zoom with me, Ryan and Jack?

It was Tanya.

Harrison was literally across the road from the Pomme d'Or Hotel, so he texted back, asking her to give him five minutes and he'd be free.

He went straight upstairs to his room and sat on the big double bed, enjoying the solitude after the noise of the press conference and before their conversation, which would have something to do with the Mannings. There was that fizz in his stomach again when he thought about them. A feeling that turned to frustration because he couldn't control the situation – and wasn't even on the same rock.

Harrison clicked on the Zoom link and waited for them to let him in.

The image of his office came up on the phone screen. Ryan was front of shot, with Tanya sitting to his left and Jack, just off camera on his right. Harrison recognised his shoes. It was good seeing friendly faces and feet.

'Y'alright, boss?' Ryan asked, smiling broadly at him.

'Fine thanks,' Harrison replied. 'How is it going your end?'

'All good. All under control,' Ryan replied, nodding sagely. Harrison had a suspicion he liked being left in charge of their tiny department, even if it was just the two of them usually.

'We were just catching up on where we are with forensics and the investigations,' Tanya spoke now, 'and we wanted to keep you in the loop.'

'They're not ready to hang you yet, witch doctor,' Jack joked from off-camera.

Tanya gave him a hard stare to show she didn't think his comment appropriate.

'OK,' said Jack, getting the vibe and becoming more serious. 'We have three ongoing investigations, as you know. First up is the Nunhead murder from 1993. The knife and blood-stained clothing, which Freda Manning so kindly donated before her death, are still being processed by the lab. We said it was a cold case so no rush; we're estimating results in the next two days. I cannot see how that is going to hurt you in the sense that even if it does place you there, you were well under age and there're no witnesses to say that you stabbed Annette Ward.'

Harrison sighed. For him, the major question to answer

was whether the flashbacks he saw of himself standing over Annette and holding a bloodied knife were true. It was his conscience, not a prosecution that was putting him on trial. He may have only been a young boy, but he would have known that it was wrong. Annette had been his friend.

'The second investigation is in Harrogate relating to the disappearance of Freda from the hospice,' Jack continued. 'Ryan said the officer investigating has been in touch?'

'Yes, he wanted to see me, but the trip over here interrupted that.'

'Well, again I don't see that you can have too much to worry about there. They will have CCTV clocking you leaving without her. Number plate recognition will pick you up on your bike heading home. What do they have which can possibly tie you in with her abduction?'

Harrison shook his head. 'Nothing as far as I can see.'

'OK, which leads us to the final case. The fire in London and Freda's death. My contact has gone quiet on this, so I'm going to have to dig a bit and go buy him a beer to see where they're at. The most worrying for you is that your helmet with your DNA was found at Desmond Manning's home address. It's that combined with your potential link to Freda's disappearance which will have them suspecting you.'

'But don't worry, boss, we're onto that one.' Ryan beamed at him again, keen to make sure Harrison didn't stress.

'Yes,' Jack said. 'Thanks to Ryan, we've been able to trace the young man who snatched your helmet from outside your flat. He took it straight to Desmond's house.'

'That's good. Will he say why he did it?'

'Mmh we don't think so, no,' Jack replied. 'When I say traced, I meant that quite loosely.'

Harrison brought his brows together, not sure what Jack was getting at.

'What Jack's trying to say is that I traced him to Desmond's house, but he doesn't appear to leave,' Ryan chipped in, keen to share his research.

'What do you mean? He's never seen coming out at all?'

'Correct, or at least, not in the same way that he went in.'

'The body in the fire? So Desmond killed him and used his body instead of his own to fool the investigators.'

'That's what we're thinking. Question is, is that where the investigation is heading or are they still convinced that the body is Desmond? Anyway, we're on it. They know Freda was killed by morphine before the fire, which was clearly a mercy act, so we've just got to persuade them that our theory Desmond staged his own death, and killed to do it, is also true. Then you're in the clear.'

'I fear that sounds easier said than done. It all depends if the investigation team comes to the same conclusions as us and we've got an advantage because we know the back story and what Desmond Manning is really like. Can we trace where he went after the fire?' Harrison was itching to get his hands on him.

'Ryan's on it. We think he took the pizza moped and headed out of London.'

Harrison felt his fists clenching at the thought, and the possibility that he might yet get to serve his own justice on Desmond. He became aware of the silence. They were all watching him for his reaction. 'Thank you all,' he said. 'I really do appreciate this.'

'No problem, mate,' Jack said. 'It's our job to make sure justice is done, that's what we all signed up for, right?' He avoided mentioning that they were also all doing it for him out of loyalty and friendship.

Harrison smiled as Jack leaned forward in his chair for

the first time, and he saw his blond head bob into the camera shot.

'I'm going to go ply my mate who's investigating the fire with beer. See if I can get a handle on where they're at. I reckon Mr Manning has played his last card,' Jack said.

Harrison smiled, but it wasn't one that warmed his face. He still had an uneasy feeling in his gut, one that warned him this wasn't over yet.

18

Harrison returned to the incident room and before continuing his trawl through the video he'd taken at the crime scene earlier that morning, he looked at the staff list and found Detective Constable Phillip Breton listed, as he'd claimed. He was with Financial Crime. There had been nothing about him which made Harrison think he had psychopathic tendencies, so that ruled out everyone who'd been at the press conference. Perhaps the killer hadn't known about it.

All around him, the team was busy chasing up the day's leads. It was more positive than yesterday, when they'd been chasing their own tails, not knowing which direction to look in.

Tracey came back, her neck tinged red – a sure sign of the stress she'd felt being interviewed.

'Pleased with how it went?' he asked her.

She shrugged. 'Seemed to go OK, what did you think?'

'Yes, it was fine,' Harrison replied.

'I take it our psychopath didn't turn up?'

'No, he wasn't there.'

'So much for him wanting to be at his own party.' She said it not in a nasty way, but out of frustration. Tracey slumped back into her chair with a big sigh and rolled her neck.

'I'm supposed to be at a parents' evening later this afternoon. Can't see that happening, can you?'

He felt for her. He only had an empty hotel room to go back to and the hope that he might get out for a run. She had three people waiting for her at home.

'I'm sure you could take an hour,' he said.

'Yeah, we'll see. My husband is going to go anyway, just in case I don't make it.'

'Want me to get you a tea?' Harrison asked. She looked like she needed a pick-me-up and he hadn't had a drink in a while either.

'Love one, please. Builders, milk, no sugar.'

Harrison stood up to leave for the canteen just as Detective Superintendent Graeme Walker came into the office with two men. One was in uniform, an older man who Harrison guessed to be the chief inspector. The other man was suited. Harrison couldn't see his face, but, even from where Harrison was standing, he could tell the suit was expensive. He didn't look like he worked for the police. The three of them stood talking for a few moments and then the man in the suit turned, giving Harrison a good look at his face.

'Who is the guy with Graeme?' Harrison asked Tracey.

She turned in her chair. 'That's the chief inspector.'

'No, the other guy.'

'Ah, that's Gary Lewis. He's a mate of the chief. They arrived in Jersey about the same time and were introduced to each other at the same welcome parties, apparently. He's a little better funded than the chief though, multi-millionaire businessman.'

'Tell me about him.'

'Gary? Why?'

'Because he was there at Harve des Pas.'

'Was he?' Tracey swung back round to look at the group of men again, as though expecting to see some evidence of Gary's visit to Harve des Pas. 'There were a lot of people there that morning.'

Harrison raised his eyebrows expectantly, waiting for her to answer his question.

She sighed.

'He has an online business selling health products and vitamins. Been here around twenty years now. Does a lot in the community, so he's alright for a multi-millionaire. Most of them keep themselves to themselves. He's one of the good ones.'

'Married?'

'Divorced. Someone said his wife and daughter moved to the States or Canada or somewhere. I'm sure there are plenty of women vying for his attention and his money.'

'How old is his daughter?'

'She was in my Lucy's class at school, so she'd be eight now.'

'Which school?'

'JCG Prep. Why all the questions?'

Harrison didn't answer. He'd already walked off and was heading towards the chief inspector and Gary Lewis. Just as the two were about to leave the incident room, Harrison held out his hand to the chief inspector. 'Chief Inspector, Dr Harrison Lane, from the Met's Ritualistic Behavioural crime unit. I just wanted to say thank you for asking me over to help with this case. It's certainly an interesting one.'

'Ah, Dr Lane, I heard you were here. Welcome to Jersey.'

He smiled warmly at Harrison. Then noticed that Harrison had looked towards Gary and smiled.

'Gary Lewis,' the man said and offered his hand to Harrison.

'Gary is a friend of mine, who has actually just stepped in to say he'd like to offer a reward for information leading to the capture of the man responsible for these dreadful killings,' the Chief explained.

Harrison shook Gary's hand, but not before he'd taken a good look at it. He had long, slim fingers for a man, with carefully manicured nails, and soft white skin, but his hands were still strong and gave Harrison's a firm grip.

The two men smiled at each other politely.

'Pleasure to meet you,' Harrison said, studying the man's face. He had the good fortune of a full head of hair still, but had dyed it black, which Harrison always felt had the effect of making men look older than if they'd left it to grey naturally. The contrast of jet-black hair and ageing skin wasn't complimentary. Gary had one of those faces that would be particularly challenging to describe to somebody. There was nothing distinctive about him. He had thin lips and fairly narrow eyes with a nose that was neither too big nor too small. The only noticeable identifier was a cleft in his chin.

'Your daughter's at school with DI Quenault's little girl, isn't she?' Harrison asked.

'Unfortunately not anymore. Her mother and I have separated. They've moved to Toronto, but I've managed to persuade them to come back for Christmas so I'm looking forward to that.' He smiled at the chief inspector as he spoke.

'I bet she was excited when she heard that there were mermaids being found in Jersey,' Harrison pressed, smiling and keeping his voice light, as though they'd just met at a social party.

'She was actually, yes.' Gary smiled at Harrison, oblivious to his motivations. 'She doesn't understand the reality behind it, just the headlines. It's made the world news. They were going to stay in Canada for Christmas because she wanted to spend it in the snow. Jersey has suddenly become more attractive again. So are you making any headway with our mermaid killer?'

Harrison seized his chance. 'You mean the mermaid butcher? His handiwork isn't as good as it looks from a distance, unfortunately.' Harrison smirked.

Anyone who knew him would know that smirking wasn't his usual style. Even Tracey, sitting watching nervously from across the room, could tell he was behaving out of character. Harrison, meanwhile, saw nothing but the man in front of him. He was watching his face intently. Waiting for the response, and he got it.

There it was. The tiniest of twitches and a very subtle change in body language.

Defensive. Insulted.

19

'You can't be serious?' DI Quenault was standing bolt upright in a defensive pose in the middle of the meeting room. The door was closed and she and Harrison were facing off.

'I am serious, yes.'

'He's a friend of the chief inspector!'

'Yes. Perfect cover, isn't it, and now he's wormed his way closer to the investigation by offering a big reward.'

'You've got no evidence, nothing to say that he has anything to do with this. I can't believe I'm even wasting my time discussing it.'

'He fits the profile perfectly.'

Tracey shook her head. 'You have met this man once and barely spoken to him.'

'I saw enough, and he gave himself away when I questioned the quality of his work. Nobody but the killer would react like that.'

'He's well connected. He's not just friends with the chief

inspector, but other senior business leaders and politicians. He's very well known in the island. People like him – he's always supporting charities. This is a crazy suggestion.'

'It's not unusual for calculating criminals to create a mask of respectability within the society they live. Psychopaths also sometimes feel a sense of duty towards the community they're a part of. It's not through empathy or any emotional attachment, purely a kind of contractual relationship, like all their relationships. Whoever has been holding these girls must have money,' Harrison argued.

'Where's the evidence, Dr Lane? There are lots of people with plenty of money here. You haven't shown me one shred of evidence – and he's not a surgeon, he's a businessman.'

'As far as you know! And he was there at Havre des Pas. I saw him and I have him on video.'

'Circumstantial at best. If you're going to accuse someone, especially someone like him, of a serious crime, you have to be absolutely sure you have the proof.' Tracey stood with her arms folded across her chest, staring up at him, determined.

'Fair enough.' He couldn't disagree with that. 'I wasn't suggesting that we arrest him, just asking that he be investigated.'

Harrison walked out of the room and over to the desk where he was still logged on, leaving Tracey open-mouthed. This wouldn't be the first time he'd had to persuade people that someone in authority and with influence was not what they seemed, and he was pretty sure it wouldn't be the last.

First off, he sat down and composed an email to Ryan, sending it from his phone rather than the Jersey police computer.

Need you to check someone out for me: Gary Lewis. He owns an online health and vitamin business over here. You're going to need to try and dig right back, probably thirty years or more. I want to know his background, his education, training and where he has lived before coming to Jersey. Then check out his estranged wife and daughter, and if you can, find out if she likes mermaids, would you?

TRACEY CAME and sat down at the desk next to him, throwing a look his way that made it clear she was annoyed. She spent five minutes on her computer and then grabbed her bag and coat and stomped out of the office without saying a word to Harrison.

He felt the icy chill in her wake, but just buried his head in the computer and carried on with his research. He hadn't come over here to make friends. He was going to find the evidence to prove Gary Lewis was the mermaid killer and save the lives of any other young women he had imprisoned before it was too late.

Harrison started by doing some research on Gary. There were plenty of business interviews and photographs from various events, but a complete absence of his personal life. He'd clearly worked hard to keep that out of the public eye. Harrison couldn't find a single mention of his wife and daughter, or anything about his own childhood prior to when he had the idea for the online business, which he'd started while working part time at a pharmacy. Harrison hoped that Ryan could work his magic. He'd never failed him yet.

One thing Harrison did manage to find was an event at which Gary was going to be giving a talk, and it was that evening at a place called the Digital Jersey Hub, starting in an hour. Harrison wanted to watch Gary in his own environment, see him interacting with people – and he also wanted him to know that Harrison was watching him. If he felt that they were on to him, he might delay his next killing. Harrison had to try something.

The Digital Jersey Hub was a modern, industrial-style co-working space furnished in minimalist steel and wood, with a great deal of glass and an open ceiling. Harrison timed it so he arrived just as the event was due to kick off. The digital space was filled with people and noise. He estimated at least eighty per cent of attendees were male, and there were a good few younger people there, wannabe entrepreneurs in their twenties. Most of them were sporting the digital uniform of jeans and trainers, and many held a slice of pizza and a beer, courtesy of the event sponsors.

Harrison slipped in and stood at the back, searching for his prey. Being tall had an advantage in crowded rooms, and he could see the top of Gary's dyed black head, talking in the middle of a group of young men who were hanging on to every word he was saying. He certainly seemed to be popular. There were a lot of people vying to talk to him, and plenty of brown-nosing going on.

Someone announced that the event was about to start and Gary, plus two other panellists, moved to the front and took a seat on the make-shift stage. He was calm and in his element. It was like watching an animal strutting in its pack on home territory. The panel was introduced and then each of the participants was asked to say a few words about themselves. Gary went first.

'Many of you will know me as the founder of VitalHealthcare. I set that up twenty years ago after a string of failed entrepreneurial attempts. I tried all sorts, from designer burgers when McDonald's were in their prime, to trying to launch my own search engine. Fail fast, and don't be afraid of it. It's how you'll learn what works and what doesn't. Rules are there to be broken. Apart from now being a multi-millionaire, I mentor and support a range of digital start-ups and I love giving back to Jersey. So, bring on your questions this evening. I'm here to inspire and motivate you to do great things.'

Quite a rousing speech, which was met with a ripple of applause from the room. But it was all just words to Harrison. He'd seen men like Gary before. Men who dressed themselves in an invisibility cloak by masquerading right in front of everyone's eyes.

People generally thought psychopaths couldn't hide in plain sight and mingle with the rest of us because we'd spot them, or they'd try to kill us, but that was wrong. The high-functioning ones, the really smart ones, were expert – and charming – manipulators. They could achieve jobs at the top of companies and politics because they were so ruthless and lacking in empathy. While only around one per cent of the general population could be diagnosed with psychopathy, in the business world it was closer to three to four per cent. It was the lower-functioning psychopaths with poorer IQs who ended up in jail fairly early on, because of their anger and lack of control.

Gary Lewis was very intelligent and clearly an expert at mimicking emotion and controlling his anger. At this stage Harrison couldn't professionally diagnose him as having an antisocial personality disorder, but even a few minutes of watching him was enough to see some of the traits he'd expect. Gary had intimated his disregard for societal rules, and he had an over-inflated view of himself, egocentric. His grandiose gesture of telling this room that he'd help them become successful was an example. Lack of inhibition was another psychopathic trait and although Gary clearly had excellent control, the fact Harrison had been able to detect his anger when he'd questioned the quality of his handiwork had shown his true colours.

As the mermaid killer, he was showing his complete lack of empathy for his victims. Perhaps he even felt he was helping them by turning them from overweight, ugly ducklings into beautiful mermaids. He recognised that they were crimes and therefore hid his actions from society, but would still feel no remorse. It was just actions taken to achieve something he wanted.

To formulate a proper diagnosis would take a lot more time and knowledge of his childhood. Harrison would be interested in sitting down and having a proper talk with Mr Lewis one day, but only after he'd brought him to justice.

Harrison stayed in the shadows at the back of the room, not far from the entrance. The conversation in front of him carried on, with Gary dominating most of the answers. Harrison calculated they were getting close to finishing – and he wanted to rattle Gary Lewis' cage.

Harrison eased his way through the crowd, towards the front where he knew the lights would be on him. His height and stature alone would be enough to ensure that Gary noticed him. Harrison lent on a table nonchalantly and watched and waited for Gary to look back to the crowd after focusing on a fellow panellist. Harrison didn't take his eyes off Gary's face. He wanted to be ready.

It took seconds for Gary to register Harrison's presence. The smile barely faltered, but there was that twitch again, followed by the clenching of his fists, and a short while later the veins in his neck rose. No one watching would have noticed the subtle changes in Gary, except for Harrison who was looking out for the tiniest chinks in his controlled arrogance. Harrison stayed in the same position, not moving his gaze from Gary's face until the talk was over and applause filled the room. Then he slipped out, knowing full well that Gary Lewis would be watching him leave, but it was Gary who needed to watch his own back.

20

H
e was in a bad mood tonight. He positively stomped into the room and started preparing the operating instruments, banging them unnecessarily. It scared them all, but it particularly scared Nicky. With each clang of metal on metal, their nerves jarred. They knew he was getting ready to do it again. Each clang meant she was one step closer to her death.

His usual gentle but cold calmness had been replaced by a hot, coiled anger which reddened his face and raised the veins in his neck.

She watched him, terrified. There was no guarantee which one he would choose, but she could easily guess at how Nicky was feeling right now. She wanted to reassure her, but her throat was too tight. He'd hear her if she whispered to her, and then what? Maybe he might choose her instead.

He stopped and leaned on the table, not moving for a few moments. Then he held his hand up and even from where she was across the other side of the room, she could see that it was shaking.

Then that was it. He walked out again, shutting the lights off and leaving them in darkness. The darkness wasn't frightening; it was the light which scared them. As the door closed, she heard a sob escape from Nicky in the cage next to her. She had been given a temporary reprieve, but it might only be an hour, or two hours. He could come back at any moment.

It was difficult to know what to say to her, how to comfort her.

'Nicky,' she'd called out into the blackness. 'Nicky, we're here,' she said again.

On the other side of her, she heard Sally call out to her too in a shaky voice. 'Nicky, we're here.'

There was another sob.

'Do you remember your dog, Baxter?' she tried. 'Remember how you used to love walking him in the fields when you were little. How you used to lie right in the middle of the biggest field, with the corn growing up around you so that nobody could see you, and just stare up at the clouds moving across the sky. Baxter used to lie next to you, never leaving your side.

'It was a blue sky, and the sun was warm on your skin. There were only a few white clouds gently floating overhead. You had one hand on Baxter, feeling his soft fur and the rhythm of his breathing, hearing his panting in one ear. There was the smell of the earth and the occasional buzz as an insect flew by. Nobody could touch you there. You were safe. Just you and Baxter in your own world, squinting up at the sun and endless sky. Remember that Nicky? You can go there now. Close your eyes and lie down and look up at that sky, feel the warmth of the sun. Baxter will meet you there.'

She stopped talking and listened. There was no more sobbing, just two warm tears trickling down her own cheeks.

21

Harrison walked to the police station the next morning. He enjoyed the exercise, and it wasn't far. Nowhere was far in Jersey. Admittedly, the wind had picked up again, and it was cold, coming from an easterly direction. Most importantly, at least it was dry with a weak winter sun trying to warm the world up.

He decided to go through town, rather than head the shorter route through the tunnel. It was far more refreshing to breathe in fresh air than car fumes, and it enabled him to pass the church where sparrows were arguing and chattering in the trees, and pigeons bobbed along in the graveyard, hoping for a morsel to eat.

It took him by the back of the States Chamber, Jersey's parliamentary building, and up the road where he saw a health and juice bar. He'd been suffering since arriving in the island, because he'd forgotten to bring any of his tea bags with him, so he went in to see if they had any. There were few luxuries in life that Harrison required, but good herbal tea bags were one of them. At the back of the shop, he found the

Pukka Tulsi Clarity tea he was looking for. The smell of fresh vegetables and fruit tempted him, and he ordered himself a Power Juice; the combination of carrot, apple, beetroot, lemon and ginger was one of his favourites.

By the time he got to the police station, it was just gone 9 a.m. and the incident room was buzzing.

'The *Daily Mail* has an interview with a woman who claims to be the mother of the first mermaid victim,' DC Peter Edwards said to him as he arrived. 'We've got a name at last.'

It was like a shot of adrenaline through the whole team. With an identity, they could now start working out the trail which led her to Jersey.

Harrison went online to look at the story. Louise Johnson was sitting in a coffee shop, dressed and wearing make-up as though she was going out for a night on the town. She was thin, painfully thin. The kind of thin that only drug addicts could achieve from the systematic and regular abuse of their bodies and desire to only put into them substances that caused harm rather than gave nourishment. She had a pained expression, looking to the camera with what she thought would be her best grieving mother's face. It served instead to make her look like the money-grabbing opportunist she was.

She clearly wasn't all that bothered about her daughter's murder, but Harrison knew she would be enjoying the attention and the nice fee she'd been paid for the story, which would no doubt end up in a syringe straight after they'd finished.

From the interview, it was also obvious that she had no idea what her daughter, Maxine, had been doing prior to ending up on the front pages of every newspaper in the world.

The *Daily Mail* had tried to dig around where Maxine had been living in the UK, but they hadn't got much. To be fair, they'd not had too much time to pull the story together. The only background they had was a school photo and an excerpt from one of her old reports. Yesterday's police appeal for anyone who might have recognised the first mermaid had obviously born fruit. Just a shame that Maxine's mother hadn't thought to speak to the police first rather than think of the money.

Harrison sent Maxine's name to Ryan. He knew the inquiry team would be tracking down where she lived and speaking to those who knew her. They'd also be trying to ascertain exactly when and how she'd left the country. What Harrison wanted to know is how she'd met Gary Lewis and what her mental state was like prior to that. He asked Ryan to look at online forums and see if he could find anywhere that she'd been hanging out. Anywhere that a calculating psychopath could have groomed her and several other girls just like her before they disappeared.

A short while later, Tracey appeared from the meeting room, closely followed by DSU Graeme Walker.

'A quick update for those of you just arriving,' Walker said to the room. 'DI Quenault will lead as I have a management meeting about budgets, but we have a name at last for our first victim, so it's progress.' With that, he nodded to Tracey and left the room.

'Right, as the boss said, our victim is called Maxine Johnson, and we're about to speak to her mother. Last-known address in Preston, Lancashire. Thanks to the *Daily Mail* who obviously paid a nice sum to her mother, we know she was pretty much estranged from both her parents and sounds like she was a bit of a loner, which explains why nobody has reported her missing. The mother had barely spoken to her in years; she's an addict, and they'd fallen out.

'While we're interviewing Louise Johnson, I need you guys to track down Maxine's landlord. See if you can get someone there to talk to her old neighbours and find out if there were any obvious associates. She's not got a social media presence anywhere, but perhaps she did once. No links to Jersey that we can tell, but we're on to Immigration now to try and find out where, when and how she left the UK and could have met her killer.'

Tracey turned to Harrison. 'Would it be worth you sitting in on the interview with Louise Johnson?'

'Yes,' he'd replied. He hadn't been sure what to expect this morning from Tracey; when she'd left yesterday, it had been obvious she was annoyed with him. He was relieved to see she wasn't going to be petty and exclude him from the investigation.

Tracey got up and started walking towards the meeting room. He took that as his cue to follow.

The logo of Preston police was visible on the screen and they could hear voices talking from way off camera.

'The Preston force have been really helpful and tracked her down for us,' Tracey said, double-checking their microphone was on mute. 'She's well known to them. Prostitution, handling drugs, shoplifting. The usual that goes with the territory of being an addict.'

The voices at the other end grew louder. 'You sit there and you should be able to see the detective in Jersey.' The thin, almost skeletal-like frame of Louise Johnson crossed the camera lens and sat in the chair directly in front. She looked from the screen to the officer, a little unsure. A uniformed torso and then head also came into view, and looked at the screen, which had the effect of staring straight down the camera lens.

'DI Tracey Quenault?' the officer asked, mispronouncing her surname, enunciating the first part like queen, and the second half with a hard t. Tracey didn't bat an eyelid. She'd heard it all before.

Tracey flicked their microphone off mute. 'PC O'Brien, thank you and good morning, Mrs Johnson. Thank you for agreeing to talk to us. I'm joined today by Dr Harrison Lane, who is helping us with the inquiry.'

Louise stared wide-eyed at them and sipped at the coffee she'd been given.

'Mrs Johnson, we are trying to catch the man who killed Maxine, and so we would be grateful for any information you could give us that would help.'

'I ain't seen 'er for like years. Not like I'm a model mum or anything, but she refused to see me. I didn't even recognise 'er in all the papers. Saw the story like, but never once thought it was my Maxine. Not until that last picture.'

'When was the last time you saw her?' Tracey asked.

Louise visibly tried to search her memory for the answer, then shrugged.

'Dunno, maybe three years. I remember it was before my fiftieth.'

'And you're how old now?'

'Errm...' She looked at her hands, as though expecting to be able to count the years on her fingers, and then up at the police officer sitting off camera.

'You're fifty-four,' the disembodied voice said.

'Yeah, yeah, fifty-four,' Louise said to the camera as though she'd known it all along. No doubt PC O'Brien had written it down so often on a charge sheet that she knew her birth date off by heart.

'And you've had no contact at all since then? No letters, emails, phone calls? Not even a text?'

Louise shook her head.

'OK. Would you know who her friends were?'

Louise pulled the corners of her mouth down. 'She didn't have none. Used to get bullied at school for being over-weight.' The memory clearly brought back an emotion, buried beneath the drug fog, because her face crumpled into anguish. 'I tried. I did try to be a good mum,' she said to them.

'We're not judging you, Mrs Johnson. We just want to find out if there's anything you can tell us about Maxine that might have led to what's happened to her.'

'Mermaids. Yeah, she loved mermaids. Used to pretend she was one when we went to the swimming pool. Had pictures all over her bedroom and her arts teacher bitched and said she wouldn't draw anything else. Strange, ain't it, that she ended up being one,' Louise said to them, completely missing the obvious connection.

THE INTERVIEW with Louise Johnson continued for another ten minutes or so before Tracey called it a day. She wasn't giving them anything useful, and was clearly struggling to get her brain to engage. She'd noticeably got more wired as the interview had gone on, so was probably in need of her next hit. Talking to her was just wasting their time.

When the call had ended, Tracey called a quick briefing to update the team.

'Sounds like Maxine had a pretty dysfunctional child-hood and was a loner who got bullied at school, mainly due to her weight. But she was obsessed with mermaids. That's the crucial link.'

'We've just had a reply from Jersey immigration,' DS Mark Le Scelleur spoke now. 'They have no record of Maxine

Johnson entering the island.'

'So she either travelled with false documents, or was smuggled in somehow.'

'Whoever is leaving the mermaids must be using a boat, so perhaps they came in across from France?' Le Scelleur suggested.

'Agreed. It's a likely scenario. If that is the case, then we should get confirmation from the UK that she left the country for Europe. It could still mean she was held in France by her killer, before being transported here finally, too. There's a lot more out of the way places to hide a group of women there, than on our tiny island.' Tracey threw a glance at Harrison. 'We have to keep our minds open to all possibilities.'

'I've spoken to her former employer,' DS Lee Prentice said now. 'He told me she'd resigned fourteen months ago. Said she seemed happy about it and told him she was going travelling. He had been a bit surprised because Maxine never seemed to have any money, but he didn't think any more of it.'

'Get hold of her bank records. Let's see if the killer paid her anything to lure her away. This makes it more likely to be a planned grooming situation, rather than an opportune kidnapping. This is good. We're making headway.'

'What about the second mermaid?' DS Prentice asked.

'Fingerprints aren't on the system and I suspect her DNA won't be either, so we'll be in the same position with her as we were with Maxine. As soon as we get the DNA profiling back, we can see if there is any connection between them in terms of geographic location. There has to be a link somewhere, besides the killer.'

'What about a dieting club?' DS Alison Holmes spoke now. 'They were both overweight. Maybe they met at Weight

Watchers or something and that's where the killer connected with them?'

'Good shout, look into that, would you? Check out any organisations and clubs in the Preston area.'

'I've finally tracked down where the lamp that was found in St Ouen was bought,' DS Le Scelleur said. 'They sell them in Jersey at the St Peter's garden centre.'

'So a link to the killer potentially being local to the island then.' Tracey nodded. 'Any idea of time frames, could we track sales and look at CCTV?'

'I've asked that but not heard anything back yet, so I might head up later to see if I can progress it faster.'

'Good, and the full report is in from the UK cosmetic surgeon Guy Kloss. More detail on what we reported back yesterday. Basically, it's one man with a medical background but out-of-date knowledge. Who was looking into the list of surgeons?'

'I'm on it,' DS Prentice replied, holding up his hand. He was a young, slim man who looked like the kind of guy who still read superhero comics and would geek out over spreadsheets. His Adam's apple bobbed up and down as he spoke. 'I've checked with the General Medical Council in the UK and they said it would be a huge list if we were to try to ask for anyone who has been on their register in the last twenty years, as you'd expect. We have started filtering local doctors, prioritising the surgeons at the hospital, and also checking alibis. No red flags so far.' He looked apologetic.

Harrison kept quiet throughout. He had made his views clear to DI Quenault, and it was up to her if she wanted to listen. She had made no mention of his theory, or any attempt to investigate it further. He was going to have to go it alone.

The briefing had just about ended when her mobile and a

couple of the other phones in the incident room began to ring.

Tracey looked at the screen and answered it. 'No. Where? OK.'

She closed her eyes and took a deep breath.

'We've got another one.'

Harrison felt sick in the pit of his stomach. A vision of Gary Lewis last night, smiling and charming in front of his audience, came into his mind. He must have left after that and gone and mutilated another young woman. How many more deaths was it going to take before they caught this man, stopped Gary Lewis?

'Where this time?' DC Peter Edwards asked, the look of shock and sadness on his face reflecting the emotions every one of them felt.

'Archirondel,' Tracey replied, throwing a glance at Harrison.

He was sat clenching his jaw muscles and balling his fists in an attempt to channel the anger and frustration which coursed through him. Three young women, cruelly murdered and their killer walking around free to do it again. This had to stop.

22

Archirondel was a small bay in the east of the island, so Harrison discovered as he looked at Google Maps en route. The sea was further out this morning, and had exposed the rocky moonscape of the shallow shoreline at low tide.

On the way, they drove past another big castle, which Tracey said was called Mont Orgueil or Gorey Castle. The medieval fortress rose up from a granite rock overlooking the pretty harbour of Gorey, as though it had erupted from the mound. Its imposing structure dominated the bay and a tiny row of brightly coloured houses and restaurants. In front of these, the protective arm of the harbour reached round to contain the little boats many of which lay stranded on their keels in the sand, waiting for the sea to return and lift them.

The narrow, winding coast road took them further east around the island, looking down on little bays and up at glass-fronted houses built into the hillside. Tracey concentrated on driving, and Harrison didn't feel like talking. He was frustrated and angry. Another young woman had lost her life, and they were no closer to arresting the killer.

The entrance to Archirondel was down a narrow lane, which had been sealed off to civilians for the investigation. Tracey pulled up at the car park and cafe in front of the small bay and Harrison immediately noticed the large granite tower, partially painted with big red and white stripes on the left hand side. It was another of the Napoleonic towers that Harrison had read about. After St Ouen and Rocco Tower, he'd looked up their heritage and history in case the killing had some connection to it.

The coastal towers had a long history of defending Jersey from attack from the sea, but there had been nothing that he could directly attribute as being a link to the mermaids. With two castles, eight forts and nearly twenty sea defence towers still standing, on the tiny nine by five mile island, he realised that wherever the killer left his mermaids, they were likely to be near to a piece of Jersey heritage.

This time, rather than place her in the middle of the sea, she'd been put on the rocks at the base of the tower.

'He's rushed this one,' Harrison said immediately to Tracey as soon as he saw the scene. 'If he's going to have made a mistake, then it will be here.'

'She wasn't found as quickly as the other two. The cafe staff don't arrive and open as early in the winter as the summer – maybe he hadn't taken that into account. The tide would have been much further in, so he's possibly brought her in by boat again, but that seems like a waste of time and energy. He could have just carried her down there.'

'I need to get a closer look,' Harrison said. 'How do you access the tower via land?'

'Up round the back here.' Tracey pointed to a track which led into an area where more cars were parked and a dirt track. It was sealed off with police tape and forensics officers had been laying stepping plates along its length.

'I need access to that path. I'll stay on the plates, but I need to see what he's left behind. Do we know who else has walked up here?'

'I'll find out.'

Tracey walked up to the uniformed officer who was manning the crime-scene tape and logging all comings and goings. While she talked to him, Harrison took a moment to bring his focus together. Anger didn't help you focus, not unless it was to do something physical like make sure he could hit Gary Lewis square in the jaw. His mind was a different matter. It needed calm. He concentrated on the sea, looking at the white waves cresting far out on the horizon, and taking deep breaths, before DI Quenault returned.

'Nobody has walked up this way that we know of. The victim was accessed via the beach because the tide had dropped, so there was no need for anyone to come this way, apart from Forensics starting to lay out the plates, but they'd have kept to these, anyway.'

'Good,' Harrison replied and turned away.

'I'll come too.'

Harrison stopped and turned back to look her in the eyes. 'I need to concentrate.'

'I'll be quiet.'

The pair of them dived under the tape, giving their names to the officer Tracey had spoken to just a few moments before.

Harrison started immediately scanning the ground. It was going to be tough deciphering footprints on a public foot-path. The only indication that they might be the killer's would be if he could follow them all the way to where the mermaid was lying, and back.

He dropped to a crouch and studied the signs on the ground. He was looking for the same footprints going in both directions, with the exception that the tracks leading to the tower would be deeper – he would have been carrying her – and the steps back would have left a shallower impression. It took Harrison a few minutes, but he finally identified them.

Harrison walked slowly, not taking his eyes from the ground. As they progressed, he was able to move faster along the track until they came to the top of the rock on which the tower sat. Harrison stopped and looked down at the young woman who was lying exactly as the others had been. She too had long blonde hair, a waspish waist and was holding a mirror. This time, she also had a few scattered grapes around her. She wasn't quite so perfect as the others. Her tail had been ripped and pitted by hungry seagulls, creating an ugly red gash where the blood from her severed legs had seeped through.

'It was seagulls that alerted the staff at the cafe,' Tracey said.

Harrison spun round and began to scan the headland around them. There were trees and private residences which would make it more difficult to see, but could potentially provide a hiding place. He doubted Gary was still there.

'What do all these sites have in common?' he asked Tracey.

'What, where they've been found? Well, apart from being beaches with cafes, I don't know. I guess they're all places popular for people who want to go swimming, or take the kids.'

Harrison nodded. That had been his observation too, but he'd wanted to ask a local in case there was something he was missing.

'So you still sticking with your theory for the killer?' Tracey's tone was terse.

'Absolutely. Trainers, around a size ten with a step length when not carrying the victim, which would indicate a height of around five feet eleven.' There was a tension in Harrison's voice, and he wanted to say something more but held back. He didn't wait for her to answer, and started to walk back the way they'd come.

Tracey, like so many before her, was left wondering how on earth he could have gleaned all that information from a dusty footpath. She followed in his wake, trying to see what he had seen.

'So why the grapes?' she asked his back.

'The third mermaid sister saw fields of grape vines when she rose to the surface.'

'So he is following the story.'

Once they reached the police cordon again, Tracey turned to the officer. 'What time did the cafe staff call this in?'

'At 8:50 a.m., ma'am. And the anonymous call was at about 8:35.'

'Anonymous call?' Tracey asked, surprised.

Harrison pricked his ears up.

'Yes, an anonymous call came in to Dispatch, said that there was another mermaid at Archirondel. By the time we got here, the cafe staff had also called us and chased away the gulls.'

'And we're sure that it wasn't any of the staff who made that original call?'

'As far as I'm aware, it couldn't have been. The caller was a man and all the staff in the cafe are female.'

'He was here watching again. Must have been mortified that the gulls had started attacking her.'

'It might not have been the killer, could have been a

member of the public who didn't want to get involved,' Tracey hit back.

Harrison looked at Tracey and said nothing. It was possible she was right, but he didn't think so.

The killer had rushed this one – but why? Had Harrison rattled him last night, wound him up and made him want to feel powerful? Or was it because he was starting to worry that Harrison was on his heels? Either way, Harrison felt a sense of responsibility, that perhaps he had made the killer take another life. This was victim number three. If his theory was right, they were halfway through the killing spree. He had to be stopped now.

23

DS Jack Salter watched the door of the pub, waiting for Detective Inspector Gordon Jacobsen to walk through it. While he'd waited, he'd had to order a drink and, mindful of the fact he was driving, he'd opted for a Diet Coke. It was a poor second best. He'd looked on thirstily as pints were pulled for other customers and passed over to eager hands. He was just watching a particularly fine-looking pint of Guinness being pulled, when a big hand slapped him on the back.

'Cotton Top,' Gordon greeted him.

Jack spun round and gave a big smile to his former colleague.

'Gopher, what's your poison?' Jack asked him, using the nickname DI Jacobsen had been known by throughout his police career.

Gordon Jacobsen had worked with Jack in Lewisham for years and, unfortunately for Jack, had given him the nickname Cotton Top because of his blond hair. Slightly older than Jack, in his early forties and with wavy brown hair and eyes, Gordon had been a good friend and colleague for many years, until a somewhat bitter divorce led him to seek a new life out of the area.

'I'll have one of the craft beers,' he replied, peering at the various names on the pump handles. Jack had been erring towards a Guinness, but after the pair of them had studied the craft beer line up for a few minutes, he joined him with a half pint of South Pacific Bitter.

'How's it going?' Jack asked him as they settled into their chairs.

'We're making headway. Need to speak to an individual, but he's currently unavailable. Things have taken a slightly different turn since I saw you last. Shifty fellow, Desmond Manning,' Gordon said and took a big sip of his beer. 'That's good.'

Jack was itching to ask him more, but he tried his drink first so he didn't look too eager. 'Refreshing, a bit citrus,' he agreed.

'You made any more headway on the historic case you were investigating?' Gordon asked him.

'We're still waiting on DNA results from a potential murder weapon, but it's nearly twenty years ago now, so I'm not holding my breath. Did you manage to get DNA confirmation for Desmond?'

'Yes and no,' he said. 'We managed to extract a small amount from an inner ear bone, but it was matching it to Desmond that was the issue. All in all, we ended up with three DNA samples taken from his car, home, and the crime scene, in addition to Freda's. There was a rather interesting family match with one, which is why we're now waiting to speak to that individual when they return to the UK.'

'Return to the UK?'

'Yes, they're currently working on a short placement.'

Jack tried not to look concerned at the high possibility
that he was talking about Harrison. Harrison's motorbike
helmet had been found at Desmond's home – there would
definitely be DNA from that, but what family match could
relate to Harrison? As far as he knew, there were no living
relatives.

'Regarding the individual in the fire, that threw up
another interesting turn of events,' Gordon continued.
'People seem to think that burning someone destroys the
evidence, but seeing as modern crematoriums with temperatures of over 1,000 degrees Celsius can't fully destroy a skele-
ton, a house fire, albeit deliberately set with accelerants, isn't
likely to. Mrs Manning's companion had received two knee
transplants. Not unusual you'd think in an older man. Only,
when we cross-referenced the serial numbers on the metal
implants with medical records, we discovered the knees
belonged to a thirty-four-year-old former bicycle courier with
arthritis.'

'Knew it was too staged and convenient.' Jack nearly
punched the air, but had to not look too excited about the
news. 'You tracked him down? Desmond, that is.'

'Not yet, we're working on it. But it certainly fits with what
we'd said before: that it was unusual to have given Freda a
morphine overdose prior to setting the blaze unless it was
someone who cared about her.'

'Looks like our friend Desmond Manning made a big
mistake picking the bicycle courier then, probably didn't
know he'd had the knee surgery.'

'No, I suspect not.' Gordon had nearly finished his pint.

'You want another?' Jack nodded at his glass.

'Can't, mate, driving and got to get back as the girlfriend's
cooking. You'll let me know as soon as you get that result on

the murder weapon, yeah? Might give us a double murder charge for Mr Manning.'

'Definitely,' Jack said. 'Hope you manage to track him down. That guy is long overdue an arrest warrant.'

'Yup, don't worry,' Gordon replied, pulling his jacket back on. 'I'll find him.'

As Jack drove home, he tried to remember the exact words Gordon had said about the DNA and an interesting family match. Was he referring to Harrison? It couldn't be Desmond and they knew the identity of the bicycle courier, so it had to be him. Maybe he'd heard it wrong or was reading too much into it. He was looking forward to telling Harrison that Desmond was now not only being hunted by them, but had a murder charge over his head; but he was worried for his friend. Was another revelation coming his way? He'd have to keep that piece of news to himself for now, discuss it with Tanya and Ryan, see if they could do some digging before he rocked Harrison's world all over again.

24

Harrison felt like a caged lion. Three women had been murdered, and the killer was still out there planning to take more lives. Gary Lewis was walking around right under their noses.

This time, Harrison might be able to place him in the area of the crime scene. Unlike the first two where he slipped in via boat, he would have had to drive her there and that would mean travelling past CCTV cameras. Harrison wasn't going to get any support from Tracey, so he had to go it alone.

While she was bringing the detective superintendent up to date, he made a beeline for DC Peter Edwards. 'DC Edwards. I don't suppose you could tell me where I get access to CCTV footage, could you?'

'Of course, Dr Lane, follow me. It's near the control room.' DC Edwards led him along the corridor to the CCTV ops room where a twenty-something brunette called Thereza looked more than delighted to have her day interrupted. Five minutes after Peter had left, Harrison already knew that she was first-generation Jersey as her parents had moved to the island from Madeira and never left; she and her brothers, who ran a decorating business with their father, all still lived at home; and her mother was a care worker. He warmed to her immediately. Friendly and straight-talking, she was the kind of young woman you could rely on to do her best. That's what he needed right now. They had to do their best to find evidence against Gary Lewis – evidence that would mean Harrison could stop girls the same age as Thereza from dying.

The first thing he did was to map the possible routes that Gary could have taken to Archirondel. One way or another, Gary would eventually show up on CCTV close to Archirondel, and from that point, Harrison could track him backwards to find out where the other girls were being kept.

Covering all the routes into and out of the Archirondel area, Harrison looked to see if a black Range Rover had passed by any of the cameras they had access to. For two hours, Thereza kept him supplied with video after video. He pored over the grainy black and white images taken the night before. He saw a black Mini estate, a red Ford Fiesta, and a white BMW 3 Series Touring, but there was no way of telling who was behind the wheel. He couldn't even see their registration plates to be able to put them in the system and check who the owners were.

He carried on looking through hour after hour of footage, right up until after he'd seen Tracey's car leave the area. If Gary had been there, he'd not driven his Range Rover. Without having more knowledge about Gary Lewis and his lifestyle, Harrison was going to struggle to get anywhere. The frustration was giving him a headache.

He thanked Thereza and decided to go for a walk to clear his head and have a screen break. He headed straight for the sea. He'd had no time to appreciate the natural beauty of the island – every trip to a beach had been a murder scene – and right now he could do with reconnecting with nature.

When he saw a large chimney looming to his right, he realised he'd come to Havre des Pas. Just as he approached the beach on the other side of the small pier and sea pool where the second mermaid had been found, his phone rang. It was Jack.

'How's it going?' Jack asked.

Harrison sighed. 'Not great. I'm sure you'd have seen the news. But I know who it is, I've just got to somehow prove it.'

'If anyone can do it, you will,' Jack replied. 'I've got some good news,'

'Go on,' Harrison replied.

'The SIO on the arson case has figured out that Freda Manning's skeletal companion was not Desmond. He's now looking for him as a murder suspect.'

'That *is* good news.' Harrison found himself smiling.

'I think he still wants to talk to you though,' Jack added. 'He didn't mention your name, obviously, but I got the impression it was you.'

'Fair enough,' Harrison said. 'Thanks, Jack, you've just made a frustrating day a whole lot better.'

'Pleasure, mate. Got to go but speak soon, yeah?'

Harrison felt a surge of relief as he reached the bottom of the little slip onto the beach. It surprised him because he hadn't consciously realised he'd been stressed about it all. He tried to think rationally and objectively about the situation, and decided that the relief was because finally somebody else was hunting Desmond Manning for murder, after nearly twenty years of Harrison being the only one. His mother's killer might not escape justice after all.

It wasn't until he'd walked past the sea pool that Harrison realised he hadn't looked at the scenery at all. His head had been totally consumed by the Mannings. He spotted some steps up to a small garden area between two buildings where he could see a couple of benches, and climbed up them. He just needed to rest for a moment.

As he sat down, a wave of emotion went through him, almost making him shudder. There had been so much death in his life. From eighteen years old when he'd lost his mother, then his grandparents, and now almost every day in his career he was faced with it. It wasn't death itself that upset him. That was a natural fact of living. It was the violence behind the dying which sometimes got to him.

This case had been particularly difficult. Three young women who had their whole lives ahead of them, subjected to torturous procedures and finally mutilated and left to die. What he found hardest to appreciate was that nobody had cared enough to look for them throughout their terrible ordeals. Gary Lewis had preyed on that fact, along with their desperate need to be noticed and liked. He'd not only taken their lives, but he'd taken their identities, totally wiping out who they were and replacing them with a fake whom their own mothers didn't even recognise.

Harrison was sure he was doing it to get his own daughter back under his control. Only a psychopath could have that motivation and then do what he'd done to another person's child. Whatever happened next, Harrison was not going to allow another girl to die.

25

If he didn't have the support of the investigating team, then Harrison needed to figure out a way to bring Gary Lewis to justice on his own. It was getting dark and there was no point going back to the incident room, so he decided to return to his hotel and come up with a plan. Probably hire a car too. First though, if he really was going to do this, then he needed information, and so he called Ryan to see how he was getting on with his research.

'Any luck?'

'Y'alright, boss? I'm making progress. I think I've found the forum where Maxine used to hang out. It's for women who fantasise about being mermaids. Would you believe it? Why would you want to be a fish? You'd be permanently cold and wet. Anyway, most of them seem virtually suicidal. They all hate their bodies and how they look and are lonely. It's like some deep sinkhole of misery and negativity. I don't get it. They want something which is just a fairy tale, totally unobtainable and so all they're doing is dragging each other down and moaning instead of doing something positive.'

'That's how he got them. He offered them their dream, a chance to make them beautiful and become the creatures of their fantasies.'

'Yeah, I can see how that would work. I've put out a few feelers and will let you know if something comes back. I reckon he'd have deleted all his posts if he was in there, but there are some things that Maxine refers to which are like she's been talking to somebody about changing her life.'

'What about background on Gary Lewis?'

'He's a dark horse, that one. I reckon he's had somebody ensure every reference to his younger years has been deleted, either that or it was never up there in the first place. Only thing I've found so far is one comment from a guy who reckons he was at uni with him. It's on an old post by an association that was advertising a talk by Gary. They'd included his biography in the post and this guy refers to that. He said, *Forgotten all your old mates at UCL Med School?* And goes on to suggest they catch up for a beer. There was no reply so Gary couldn't have seen it.'

'That's crucial, Ryan,' Harrison said. His heart had jumped when he heard it. Something tangible at last. He'd trained as a doctor.

'Yeah, I'm trying to track down the dude who wrote it and also chasing UCL to see if they can confirm if he studied there. On it, boss, I promise.'

'Thanks, and can you get his address for me? I'm going to need to pay him a visit.'

'Don't the team there have that?'

'Let's just say that they haven't quite come round to my way of thinking about him yet.'

'You won't do anything stupid, right?'

'No, Ryan, I won't.'

. . .

HARRISON HAD to admit that Ryan's concern was probably quite reasonable. He was fired up by his conviction that Gary Lewis was their man and desperate that he prove it before anyone else got killed. It was at times like this that he came close to overstepping the line. He was going to have to restrain himself from going straight round to Gary's house and tearing the place apart to find any clues as to where he was keeping the girls – preferably after knocking Gary Lewis out cold.

To calm himself down, he went straight up to his room and got changed into his running kit before heading out the door again and crossing the main road to the cycle path and footpath that ran all along the avenue. A highway of fresh air straight off the beach. It was just what he needed; a long, straight stretch that he could power down, pushing his body to go faster, his muscles to extend and his lungs to fill deeper.

The tide was now high and the sound of the traffic was muffled by the crashing of the waves against the seawall. Every now and then, a wave would top the wall and splash down in front of him, or occasionally hit him. The inky-black sea was lit by a large white moon and he could see the bay stretch out in front of him in a gentle curve. The sea seemed rougher now, and the wind was blowing straight off it. It carried the smell of the salt and seaweed, and a seemingly endless ocean that cared nothing for his thoughts or the young women who were dead or waiting to die.

Harrison focused on the raw natural elements around him, trying to let them envelop him, and cancel out the image of the two young women he'd seen lying on metal autopsy tables; or the seagull-pecked body of the latest victim abandoned on a rock. He tried hard to not think about the other girls he was convinced were waiting their turn. Harrison ran all the way to the end of the avenue where a burger bar was lit up and groups of young people were hanging out, making a can of coke and a burger last for two hours. His lips tasted salty from the sea, but he wasn't hungry yet. The anger he felt at Gary Lewis and the difficulties Harrison faced proving the man was guilty had served to ruin his appetite.

Harrison turned and ran back again. His muscles were getting tired now, so he had to push them hard, and almost welcomed the pain which seared through his lungs and in his quads and glutes. He felt alive, pumping the oxygen around his body and to his brain. It would help him sleep – and it would help him think. He had to find a way to build a case against Gary Lewis.

Harrison jumped straight into the shower as soon as he got back to his room. He stood under the hot water, enjoying the heat flowing over his solid muscles and, finally, the endorphins coursing through his system and round his brain started to relax him.

He'd literally only just stepped out when there was a knock on the door. Throwing a towel around his waist, he dripped over to see who it was, presuming it might be House-keeping come to see if his bed needed turning down.

It was difficult to know who looked more surprised, Tracey, who was treated to a half-naked vision of Dr Harrison Lane with water still dripping off his chest muscles and six-pack, or Harrison himself. DI Quenault won the most embarrassed prize, turning a bright shade of red.

'DI Quenault, apologies. I wasn't expecting you. Have I missed a message? I've been out running.' Although surprised, Harrison seemed fairly oblivious to the fact he was only wearing a towel around his waist.

Tracey recovered her composure, but her voice was less authoritative than usual. 'My apologies. I wanted you to meet someone and thought I'd check if you were in on the off chance you could hear what he has to say.'

Considering how they'd left things when he'd suggested that Gary was their killer, he was surprised by the change of heart.

'Have you eaten?' she asked.

'No,' Harrison replied.

'Perhaps you could join us for dinner in the Harbour Room?'

'Of course. I'll get dressed and meet you in five minutes.'

Harrison closed the door and wondered who it was that she seemed so eager for him to meet. If it was somebody who was going to try to persuade him that Gary Lewis was a good guy and had helped him turn his life around thanks to some charitable donation, then he doubted he'd last through the starter. The run had relaxed him. The last thing he wanted was to get wound up again.

HARRISON WAS true to his word and arrived in the Harbour Room restaurant entrance just a few minutes later. He'd only towel-dried his hair, and his skin still glowed fresh pink from the double combination of the exercise and hot shower.

He spotted Tracey immediately and walked over to join her at a table where an elderly man was sitting with her. He looked like he might be from the Mediterranean area, and Tracey introduced him as Roberto Da Silva, which suggested Portugal or Madeira.

Harrison could tell that Roberto clearly hadn't spent his career sitting in an office. For his age, he still had a good physique, and his skin told of a lot of time spent outdoors.

'Thanks for coming,' Tracey said to Harrison. 'I wanted

you to meet Roberto because I think he has something to tell you that you might find interesting.'

Harrison raised his eyebrows and looked at Roberto.

'I was gardener at Melrose House, over twenty years, 1974 to 1996.'

Harrison shot a glance at Tracey.

'Melrose House is currently the residence of Gary Lewis,' she lowered her voice, flicking her eyes around the other diners to ensure there was nobody there who might have a vested interest in their conversation.

Harrison nodded.

'The housekeeper, she worked there since just after war.' Roberto continued. 'Good lady. Looked after Mr Downey. She told me she seen secret underground room, under house. Mr Downey built it to hide his paintings, worth a lot of money. He was scared Germans or Russians would invade again, so created safe room.'

'Surely it would be on the plans when the house was sold?' Harrison asked them both.

Roberto shook his head. 'Mr Downey built it straight after war when planning not organised. He lived on his own and died with no children. A cousin was left house and he sold it and all contents. The room was sealed. We looked, but could find nothing. No way in. The cousin never came here. I lost my job and Mr Lewis moved in.'

'Did the housekeeper not know where to find it?'

Roberto shook his head. 'It was secret door. She'd seen it open once and Mr Downey said he locked it. He told her when he dying. She couldn't find it after, and neither could we. She said he wanted it to stay hidden. Called it his secret he'd take to grave.'

'Whereabouts did you look?'

'There only one place. A wine cellar with stairs from hallway. You go down and it is small room. But somewhere behind is big room. Stretching under whole house.'

'Surely there must be some kind of ventilation system then?'

Roberto shrugged. 'I knew those grounds well. I never saw anything, but there was area of garden Mr Downey didn't want tidied. He said it had to be left wild. Maybe it there.'

Harrison sat back in his chair and thought. 'You definitely believed the housekeeper? She couldn't just be repeating a rumour?'

Roberto shook his head violently. 'No, no no. She was honest woman. She saw it.'

'How did you find Roberto?' Harrison asked Tracey.

'Something you said back at the station reminded me of a story one of my husband's aunts had told me. She's in a care home now, but thankfully still got all her marbles. I went round to ask her, not even sure whether I'd remembered it right or if it was the same house. She put me on to Roberto and I invited him out for dinner.'

Tracey smiled broadly at Roberto, who was busy scanning the menu.

When the waiter came to ask them for their dinner choices, Harrison found he'd rediscovered his appetite.

It was a big relief to find that DI Quenault hadn't ignored his suspicions. She was a dark horse. He'd been sure that she'd not believed him. After dinner, she called a taxi for Roberto and she and Harrison had one last drink together so they could talk more freely about the case.

They were sat by the glass doors which led to a balcony that overlooked Liberation Square. Both of them drank chamomile tea.

'It wasn't that I didn't believe you as such, it's just we're going up against someone who is incredibly well connected. I don't fancy ruining my career. I don't know you, Harrison. I hear that your reputation is excellent and that you get results, but I've barely known you more than forty-eight hours. I'm not going to throw my career away on a stranger's gut feeling.'

'It's not a gut feeling,' Harrison said. 'Although actually gut feelings are valid instincts that should be listened to. It's your body's way of telling you something that you brain just hasn't quite caught up with. I worked with a lot of psychopaths when I did my training and gained experience in prisons. If you observe them for a long time, you get to know the kinds of behaviours and characteristics to look for.

'I said all the way along that the killer would be at the crime scene, watching us discover his creation. He was there at Havre des Pas, sitting in his car calmly watching. He could very easily have been in St Ouen doing the same thing. Then he turned up at the station and wanted to offer a reward.'

'Are you always this suspicious about people's motivations? He could have just been upset by what he saw at Havre des Pas and been inspired to help. He's known for it. There was a fire at a family's house a couple of years ago, and they lost everything just before Christmas. He gave them a load of money so they could stay in a hotel and get presents for the kids and stuff. He's a local hero.'

'How did the fire start?'

'What?'

'Was there an investigation into how the fire started?'

Tracey thought for a moment. 'I don't know actually, the fire brigade would have dealt with that. I'm not aware any criminal investigation went on, but then it just may not have crossed my desk. Why?'

Harrison raised one eyebrow and took a sip of his tea before replying. 'Psychopaths like to play God.'

'Well, we need to keep this line of inquiry to ourselves.

Even with Roberto's story, we don't have any proof or any concrete evidence to take to Graeme, let alone the chief inspector. We need a lot more than just an old gardener's memory.'

'I know,' Harrison replied. 'But I think he studied medicine at UCL. That puts him firmly in the frame. Hopefully we'll get that confirmed tomorrow.'

'Really? That certainly changes things. Good.'

Their conversation was interrupted suddenly by a hammering against the balcony doors. The wind was driving hail stones against the glass and they were bouncing off and piling up on the balcony.

'Bloody weather,' said Tracey. 'I had to park my car up the hill. I'll get soaked. Mind you, they did say there was a storm coming in.'

'Good,' Harrison replied.

She looked at him, a bit surprised.

'Good that I'll get soaked?'

'No. Good that it's stormy. He won't kill tonight if he can't leave them looking beautiful. He needs good weather for that. We've got a short reprieve until we can put together a case and get a search warrant.'

Tracey waited another ten minutes or so for the hail to die down before dashing off to find her car. Harrison returned to his room feeling exhausted. He felt a lot better now that he was making progress and they potentially knew where the girls were being held, and he thanked the weather for ensuring that tonight at least they could sleep easy knowing there wouldn't be another dead mermaid on a beach in the morning.

He was about to turn off the light for sleep when a text came through from Ryan.

Found a woman who was groomed by
mermaid killer in the same forum as Maxine.
She nearly left to meet him in France, but
decided against it because of her cat. She's
happy to talk. Have also found photo of wife.
You're going to want to see it, will forward all
in morning.

Harrison nearly punched the air with relief; it was going to be a huge help to the investigation. He texted Ryan back to say thank you and sent one to Tracey, then lay back on the bed. He was ready for sleep. Tomorrow he was going to stop Gary Lewis and end his sick game.

26

'Got you some caffeine,' Tracey said to Harrison as soon as he arrived in the incident room.

'Sorry, I don't drink it,' he replied, though he appreciated the thought.

'No problem. I need all the coffee I can get.' She reached over and grabbed it without a second thought. 'By the way,' she added, dropping her voice. 'That fire I told you about? Fire brigade said it was arson, but nobody was ever charged.'

Harrison hmphed, but said nothing more. His phone pinged with a message, and he took it out to read.

When he looked up, he had a huge smile on his face. He turned his phone round and showed her the screen. It was from Ryan.

> UCL has confirmed Gary Lewis studied to be a doctor with them for five years.

'Yes!' Tracey exclaimed, causing a few of the other officers in the room to look up.

'I think we've got enough to put this out to the whole

team a bit later, but I might just need to have an awkward conversation on the management floor first.'

THE WOMAN who Ryan had found from the mermaid forum, Lauren Borman, had agreed to talk to them via a Teams call that morning. Until yesterday, she'd not put two and two together and realised that the Jersey mermaids were related to Maxine and the group. Most of them didn't use their real photos as an avatar. Hers was her cat, and so she'd not recognised the photographs of Maxine that had appeared in the media. It was only when Ryan linked her own chats to Maxine and told her she'd disappeared and then turned up dead on a Jersey beach, that she'd realised who she was.

When Lauren appeared on screen, Harrison could see why Gary had chosen her. She had an awkward way about her which spoke volumes about her lack of confidence and self-esteem. Although she seemed thinner than the other girls must have been, she still clearly struggled to keep the weight off. Gary had chosen a certain type of young woman, one he could mould to how he wanted her to be, like human clay. She normally had long, light- brown hair, but today it was streaked with purple. She looked nervous, not surprising considering the subject of their conversation and the fact most people were a little nervous when talking with the police.

Harrison watched Tracey put her at ease by chatting about the cat, which lounged on the sofa behind Lauren.

'What's his name?'

'Rudi.'

'He's a big fella. We used to have a cat when I was little, but ours was a lot smaller than him. He's like a fluffy tiger.'

Lauren giggled. 'He's a Norwegian Forest. Very lazy and

has to be brushed nearly every day. I'm just his house servant.'

'Well, he's lovely.' Tracey smiled. 'We won't keep you from him for long. Thank you for talking to us today. Would you mind telling us about Maxine?'

'She was a nice girl,' Lauren said. 'She was just like me. Overweight, fed-up, lonely. I remember she talked about doing all sorts of things with her life, but she could never do it because she didn't have any money or support. She was depressed.'

'Tell me about how this man approached you?' Tracey asked.

'I wasn't even sure it was a man at first. His profile name was *MermaidCreator* so I assumed he was another woman initially. Then he started to say that he could help me. You know, I'm not stupid. I know there're loads of these guys from overseas who do scams and stuff, but it wasn't like that. He sent me money for Rudi's vet bill when he got bitten by another cat, and he was smart, funny, and totally charming. He seemed to understand why we all wanted to be mermaids and get away from reality.'

'How long did this go on for?'

'Errm, we started talking at the start of the year before last and I was going to meet him in the November.'

'Meet him?'

'Well, it was a bit more than that. He told me to leave my job, give up my flat and go and live with him. Said he was a plastic surgeon and he would help me become the mermaid I'd always wanted to be. He never talked about losing your legs and having a fish tail. I thought he meant I could become a professional mermaid.'

'A professional mermaid?' Tracey queried.

'Yeah, you know other women do it. They wear fake tails

and learn to swim properly like mermaids, and then do parties and appearances. It's huge in America.'

'You can make money that way?'

'Of course, there're loads of mermaid impersonators. He said he could make me the best.'

'So what happened?'

'He sent me money to get a Eurostar ticket to France. Told me to hand in my notice on the flat and get rid of all my stuff. He said I could bring a couple of suitcases, but he'd buy me everything I needed. I nearly went. I started packing up but I couldn't leave Rudi, so I sent him the money back and never heard from him again.'

'Could you let us have the bank account information that he used?'

'Yeah, sure.'

'Did you ever see a photograph of this man, or speak to him in real life?'

'He did send me a photo once, but it probably wasn't really him. I never spoke to him on the phone or on video. We did everything online.'

'Was there anything he said that could link him to Jersey, or gave you any idea as to his real identity?'

Lauren was quiet for a while. They could see she was trying to remember something. 'There was one thing. He said he had a daughter, and she totally loved mermaids. I was surprised because he'd never even mentioned a wife or partner before then. Our relationship had never been romantic or anything. He never once made any suggestions. It was like he wanted to be a father figure.

'I'd also kind of assumed that he was wealthy. Just by the way he talked about money, he was someone that didn't need to think about it. Do you know what I mean? So when he mentioned his daughter, it made me wonder why he wanted to help me if he had her to take care of already. I think in the frame of mind I was in then, I'd still have gone through with it, if it hadn't been for my Rudi.'

'Your cat saved your life, Miss Borman,' Tracey said to her.

'I know, and I've joined Weight Watchers since and lost three stone. Life's not so bad now.' She sniffed, tears escaping her eyes and running down her cheeks. 'He seemed so lovely, really he did. Poor Maxine.'

When they'd finished the phone call with Lauren, Tracey sat in the chair for a few moments, not saying anything. Harrison knew she was running something through her mind and so he'd waited, giving her time.

'OK. Let's do it? Let's go and tell the chief inspector and Graeme. We need to get this out in the open so we can investigate properly.'

Harrison jumped up before she could change her mind.

'MORNING BOTH.' Detective Superintendent Graeme Walker smiled at the pair of them as they walked into his office. 'How's progress, Tracey? We getting anywhere?'

'Yes, I believe we are. I think we have a suspect.'

'That is excellent news. Excellent. Harrison, I'm sorry that we may have got you over here on slightly false pretences. We were so sure, after the first murder, that it was some kind of cult, but your input has been invaluable.'

'It's fine, just because we're now looking at a psychopath as opposed to some kind of cult, doesn't mean that there isn't an element of ritual behind the crimes. In fact, it was his ritualistic way of presenting the bodies that allowed me to work out the motivation behind the killings. Rituals come in many forms, they're not just Satanic or Pagan practices.'

'Good, well glad you've been here to help. So come on, tell me about our suspect?'

'It's Gary Lewis,' Tracey replied and then waited for the reaction.

The detective superintendent's face didn't hide his shock. 'What? The vitamin millionaire guy?'

'Yes.'

'He's just put up a reward for information leading to the killer's capture.'

'I know,' Tracey replied, but her voice sounded less confident.

'He is a controlling psychopath. The closer to the investigation and investigators he is, the more likely it is he can exercise some control,' Harrison stated. 'I bet he has asked how we're getting on?'

DSU Walker raised his eyebrows to show Harrison had got it right.

'You realise that if you're wrong about this, it's going to reflect very badly on you, Tracey?'

'Yes, sir,' she said quietly.

'Tread carefully. He knows a lot of people and has deep pockets. If you screw this up, then it won't just come down on your head. I take it you're going to inform the chief?'

She nodded. 'Right now.'

'OK, good luck.'

HARRISON FELT her breathe again as they walked out of DSU Walker's office.

'Well, that went better than I expected,' she said to Harrison.

'He trusts you.'

'Let's hope it's not misguided then. We've got the tough

one now. I don't think we're going to get quite such a good reception.'

They walked up to the management floor and waited to be called in to see the chief inspector. Harrison noticed Tracey was rubbing at her leg and jiggling in her seat. He could see the stress building up in her. The chief had just opened his office door to call them in when a text buzzed on Harrison's mobile. He quickly looked at it as they walked in.

The chief inspector greeted them both warmly, and Harrison wondered if they'd be parting company on such good terms. His office had an excellent view towards Havre des Pas. With the winter sun streaming in through the windows, it was a pleasant space to work.

Tracey was desperate to get it over and done with, so launched straight in. 'We've identified a suspect in relation to the mermaid killings.'

'Excellent news.' He beamed at her.

'It's Gary Lewis, sir.' Tracey almost ducked as she said it.

'Gary Lewis? You're not serious?'

Tracey nodded solemnly.

'So you're telling me that one of my good friends is mutilating young women and turning them into mermaids? Have you lost your minds? Why would Gary do that? He's a man with everything he needs; a beautiful house, money, a successful business, life's good. Why would he have any interest in doing this?'

'His life isn't perfect, his wife has taken his daughter away from him,' Harrison replied. 'You heard him say that she wanted to stay in Canada for Christmas to be in the snow, but when she heard about the mermaids being found here, she changed her mind.'

'So now he's killed several women just to get his daughter to fly over for Christmas? Have you not read today's *Jersey*

Evening Post?' The chief picked up the local paper from his desk and waved it at them both. 'He's just donated fifty thousand pounds to support men with drug and alcohol addictions in the island – look. The guy bends over backwards to help the community. Does that sound like a psychopath to you?'

The CI looked from Harrison to Tracey in the hope of finding at least some semblance of sense in one of them.

'Actually, yes. It's not uncommon for high-functioning psychopaths to appear to be altruistic in order to cover their true characters,' Harrison said.

He glanced at the photograph in the newspaper: a smiling Gary shaking hands with the head of a drug rehabilitation service following his tour of the facility, which would be seeing a room named in his honour.

'Did you know that he'd trained as a doctor and was going to become a plastic surgeon? He ducked out of it when he first had the idea of the business,' Harrison added.

The CI didn't answer the question, but the look on his face told them both that it was news to him. He stood up from his chair and paced in front of the windows.

'Tell me you've got more than that? This is all circumstantial.'

'He's been hanging around the investigation. That's classic controlling behaviour. He's keeping an eye on how well we're progressing and I saw him at Havre des Pas.'

'So where's he keeping them?'

'We think at his home, sir. I spoke to a former groundsman at Melrose House. He used to work for the previous owners about twenty years ago. Said that he'd been told of a secret room in the house. It was some kind of storage area for the original owner who built the property. He was an art collector, paranoid about the Germans coming back and stealing his pictures after the occupation, and so he built this secret underground strongroom,' Tracey replied.

'And has anybody ever been in it?'

They both shook their heads.

'So it's probably another one of those post-occupation stories that has been embellished and retold but has absolutely no grounding in truth.'

'Did you ever meet his wife?' Harrison asked now, quietly.

The CI looked at him, clearly thinking.

'Only briefly, maybe once or twice. I didn't know her well. He used to attend most events on his own because she would be at home with their daughter.'

Harrison swiped open his phone and went to the text he'd received just as they were entering the office. He tapped on the photograph that it contained and turned it around for the CI to see.

'This is Mrs Lewis.'

The chief's face said it all. He was staring at a woman with long blonde hair, who looked as though she could have been one of the mermaid victims. The resemblance was striking.

'OK, OK. You do what you have to do.' He said, shaking his head. 'Keep the investigation as far away from me as possible. It's obviously a conflict of interest. I don't want to know any details. But so help me, if you're wrong and I not only lose a good friend, but he decides to sue our arses, then DI Quenault I suggest you book yourself a seat on the same plane Dr Lane gets on back to the UK.'

'Well, that actually went better than I'd expected!' Tracey said to Harrison as they walked out, a look of mock chasteness on her face. 'Let me see that photograph of the wife again? I can't believe how similar she looks. Why has she not noticed it too? She must have seen the photographs; the mermaids went global.'

'People are blind to it. What we see in the mirror is not how others see us. We always look different in photographs than we expect, don't we? And while she might see a resemblance, she won't pick up on just how similar they are to her.'

'It's sick. She's going to be horrified when she realises. Right, let's go and tell the rest of the team and work out how we're going to bring this one home.'

27

I t had just gone 4:30 p.m. and Harrison walked back into the incident room after having gone to the canteen to get a bottle of sparkling water. Tracey almost ambushed him.

'Dr Chaudhry has found a partial fingernail inside the fish tail of the Archirondel mermaid. It has to be the killer's.' She beamed. 'You said he'd make a mistake, and he has. We're going to get him. I'm arranging to ask a selection of men who are doctors and surgeons to take a DNA test to eliminate them from our enquiries.'

Harrison raised an eyebrow.

'Yes,' replied Tracey. 'We'll ask Mr Lewis. Now that we know he trained as a doctor, we have a legitimate reason, and if he refuses, then we get tougher.'

'When do you think we'll get a search warrant?'

She shook her head.

'Not yet. We've not got anything on him that would be considered strong evidence. It's all circumstantial. He would fight it with a whole team of expensive lawyers. If we can match his DNA, then it's game over.'

'I'd like to come with you to his house when you go and ask him.'

'I hadn't expected anything else,' Tracey replied, smiling.

MELROSE HOUSE BEGAN at the roadside with a high wall and a large set of wooden gates.

'Likes his privacy,' Tracey commented as they pulled off the road in front of the locked gates. She got out of the car and pressed the intercom panel to get attention.

'Yes,' a man's voice asked via the speaker.

'It's DI Tracey Quenault from States of Jersey police. I'm after Mr Gary Lewis, please? I just want to have a word?'

The disembodied voice didn't reply, but the gates silently swung open and so Tracey got back in the car and carried on up the winding drive to the house.

It was clear that Mr Lewis must still employ a gardener because the grounds were quite extensive and well looked after. All the bushes and shrubs were trimmed and shaped, the lawn neat and thick, and the flower borders weed-free. The stormy weather had caused some debris to have blown down from the trees and so the gardeners couldn't have been there that morning. Harrison suspected that Gary would avoid having people in the house and grounds unless during clearly defined hours, so that they couldn't bear witness to anything he shouldn't be doing. Control of his environment would be paramount.

Security lights flooded the drive and gardens as they made their way towards the house, all motion activated.

'Must cost a bloody fortune to run all these lights. You could play a football match under them,' Tracey muttered.

There were no other cars to be seen outside the house, but just around the side Harrison could see a four-door garage which would undoubtedly house the black Range Rover he'd seen Gary in before, and possibly another car or three. The house itself was an attractive granite building, never built to be a working farm like so many other properties he'd seen, but clearly designed for the landowner with wealth. A pillared porch was lit up by two carriage lamps and as soon as they'd scrunched to a halt in front, the door opened, allowing them to see inside a black-and-white tiled hallway.

Gary Lewis was framed by the light coming from inside. It was difficult to tell what he was thinking about their arrival. Understanding psychopaths, Harrison knew it was unlikely that the man would be fearful. He'd think himself untouchable, and this was just another match in his game of cat and mouse.

'DI Quenault,' he said, smiling only with his mouth and stepping down the steps to greet her with an outstretched hand. 'To what do I owe this pleasure?' Finally, he pointedly turned to look at Harrison. 'And Doctor Lane, isn't it? Welcome to Melrose House. Please do come inside out of this awful wind. If I'm not mistaken, it's going to rain again tonight and they're predicting gale force eight by midnight.'

Harrison could see past the plastic welcome. The forced smile and pleasantries came from a man with no soul. They followed him into the house.

'I'm afraid I only have staff during the day, but if you would like a cup of tea or coffee, I'm sure I could manage to work out how to use the kettle?'

The question was primed to get them to say no; he didn't want to leave them alone. That was obvious.

'No, we're fine, thank you,' Tracey replied. 'You have a lovely home, Mr Lewis.'

'Why thank you, yes it is quite something, isn't it? I always say that we are just custodians of houses like this. One day I will pass it on to someone else.'

Harrison hoped that day would come sooner rather than later, when he was sent down for life.

'Come through to the drawing room. Is this about the reward I've offered? I hope you're here to tell me that the killer has been caught and I need to pay up?' The charming lies oozed from his pores like pus from a carbuncle. It turned Harrison's stomach.

'No, I'm afraid not. But we found some evidence on our latest victim and we're asking a small group of men in the island to volunteer to be DNA tested so that we can eliminate them from our enquiries.'

'And I'm in this small group?' Gary replied, but Harrison could tell he was feigning surprise. He'd been expecting this.

'If you don't mind, yes. We are asking all men with past medical training to come forward to be tested and we understand that you studied medicine at UCL.'

'That's well researched. I did indeed train in medicine, it's how I came up with the idea for my business.' He smiled at them both and looked straight into Harrison's eyes. 'I don't like to advertise it though because I want to inspire all young people to achieve and if they think that I have a degree in medicine after going to an excellent university, then it might somehow make it less achievable for them.' He looked back to Tracey now. 'You don't need qualifications to make a success of your life. Don't you agree?'

'How noble,' Harrison replied sarcastically.

Gary turned back to him again, a little too sharply for his usual cool response. He paused a moment, staring him straight in the eyes. Harrison knew what he was doing. He was trying to anger and unnerve him.

For a few moments, the pair of them stared at each other, neither blinking nor budging. Harrison fought the urge to land a fist in the smug psychopath's face. He could almost feel the satisfying crunch as it connected, but he refused to allow the man to wind him up. Gary's eyes were cold and dark, with a hint of steel that gave away his true intention. Harrison fought them with the fire of a passion to see justice done. Gary Lewis was going to get nowhere trying to intimidate him.

'Thank you,' Gary said calmly, smiling again and breaking the stand-off. He turned to Tracey. 'Quite ironic really, isn't it, that I am a suspect in the murder investigation that I've put up a reward for. So what do you need me to do?'

'I didn't say you were a suspect, Mr Lewis,' Tracey replied sweetly.

Harrison liked her style.

'Ah, so what do you call it then in your lingo, a person of interest perhaps?'

Harrison could tell he was enjoying every minute of this.

Tracey ignored the veiled goading. 'The DNA test is all very simple and won't take long. I just need you to sign some consent forms first and you can read our privacy and sample retention policies. Your DNA will only be used for the purposes of this case.'

Gary nodded.

While Tracey and Gary discussed the forms and she got the swab ready, Harrison looked around the room. Whatever was in here would be the public face that Gary Lewis wanted the world to see, a mask of respectability that was only millimetres deep.

He had several paintings on the wall. They wouldn't be

Harrison's choice; they were far too modernist and devoid of human emotion. One was just coloured circles on a white background. It looked as if a secondary school student could have produced it, but Harrison knew it would probably be a great modern artist whose works were worth tens of thousands, if not hundreds.

On one side of the room was a large bookcase. Even from where he sat, Harrison could see that Gary had organised the books alphabetically. His mind liked order and control. Chaos was not allowed, even on his bookshelves. Also on the shelves were some photographs. Photographs of Gary with a young girl, presumably his daughter. His wife was notable by her absence, although that in itself wasn't unusual, seeing as they were going through a divorce. Harrison wanted to get a closer look at the photographs. They were all taken on different beaches.

'You must be looking forward to your daughter coming over,' Harrison said to him, standing up and walking over to the photos.

Gary watched him closely. 'Yes. I am.'

'When is she arriving?' Harrison pressed, turning and smiling at him, but not before he'd noticed the mermaid doll in Gary's daughter's hand from the photograph in St Ouen.

Gary paused a moment before replying, perhaps weighing up whether he should share that information. 'Next week. Her school breaks up early for Christmas.'

Next week was a clear deadline for Gary to finish what he started and get ready to receive his daughter. It was also a clear deadline for them. Presuming there were other girls, they were going to have to be gone before his family arrived.

'Could I ask you to look at me a moment please while I do this?' Tracey asked, taking the swab out of its wrapper. 'And open your mouth for me.'

Gary reluctantly turned back to her. It gave Harrison the chance he'd been looking for. He took his phone out of his pocket and quickly took a snap of the photographs. If he wasn't mistaken, there was one of them on the beach at St Ouen, one at Archirondel, and one in the sea pool at Havre des Pas. The other three he didn't know, but they could be the next drop-off points and, if that was the case, they'd be able to get ahead of him. If they had highly visual patrols on the beaches and made a public show of the fact they knew he was going to choose those locations, it could throw his plans out of synch.

Harrison went to sit back down and studied Gary while Tracey finished the test. He looked exhausted. Despite the man's blasé attitude, Harrison could tell that the nocturnal events of the past week had taken their toll. He was fit and healthy for his age, but he wasn't a particularly strong man.

The effort of what he had done to those women, coupled with the act of getting them to the location and posing them in the early hours of the morning, without being seen, must have been exhausting. Perhaps that was one reason why he chose Archirondel: because it was easier to drive to and access via land rather than the rigmarole of getting her into a boat, sailing round the coast in dark seas, hoisting her off again and returning home. It was hours of work. He could have barely slept. The contrast of his pale skin with his dyed-black hair had become even more pronounced.

'Been working long hours?' Harrison asked him.

Gary narrowed his eyes slightly as he looked across to Harrison.

'Yes. Always busy, but I can't complain,' he said smoothly.

The DNA test didn't take long and, within a few minutes, Tracey was standing up and thanking him for his cooperation.

'It's no problem at all. Anything that helps find your man.' He smiled at her again, the grimace of a shark trying to fool the fish that he was their friend. Then he turned to Harrison.

'Dr Lane, what is your role in this DNA exercise? Are you assessing if any of your suspects are crazy?' His tone was haughty and condescending.

Harrison smiled broadly at him. 'Not at all, Mr Lewis. I'm Tracey's bodyguard, that's all.' He smiled again.

They said their goodbyes and Gary Lewis closed the door on them.

Once they were safely back in the car and out of earshot, Tracey turned to Harrison. 'Well, that seemed to go smoothly.'

'Did you notice his reaction when you asked him to take a DNA test and told him about the evidence?'

'Yeah, he didn't seem surprised or bothered.'

'That's right, I think he knew we were coming.'

'You mean you think someone tipped him off? I'm one hundred per cent sure that the chief wouldn't do that.'

'No, I'm not suggesting he would. Psychopaths make up a much larger percentage of the prison population in comparison to the general population. That's because generally they are risk-takers, and tend to be more impulsive, so they stand out. Yet the traits of a psychopath can't all be seen as negative. Someone like Gary, who is highly intelligent, has clearly studied the society he is a part of in order to optimise his success. He will look at risk slightly differently. He's learned to understand the boundaries in order to hide in plain sight, but that kick he gets from knowing how close he flies to the line is what keeps him entertained. I think he saw that we were starting to get closer, and he's just deflected it.'

'I don't understand what do you mean?'

'The third victim seemed rushed. I don't think he

intended to kill her that day, but he needed a way to deflect the inquiry. He knows full well that the convenient piece of evidence we've just found on victim three is not going to match with him.'

'But I took the swab – he couldn't have faked that.'

'Yes, you did. But what if the fingernail isn't the killer's?'

Tracey was silent for a few moments. 'I wish you'd thought of that before we did all this.'

'I'm sorry. It was his reaction to our being there. He's a total control freak. If we had just told him that he'd made a mistake and accidentally given us some evidence, he wouldn't be worried as such, but he would have been angry at himself for making a mistake. There was no reaction at all.'

'Maybe you're giving him too much credit.'

'Maybe,' Harrison replied, but he didn't think so.

'They're on standby to test these results ASAP at the lab, so I'm just going to hope we get a match tomorrow, and while these gale force winds carry on, it should keep Gary Lewis at home until we can arrest him.'

Harrison looked out the window at the trees bending and bowing in the gusty winds. He didn't share Tracey's positivity. Gary's reaction had been the conceited behaviour of a man who knew he had nothing to fear. It wasn't over yet.

28

There were just two of them left now, and she knew it could be any time that he came for her. She was next. In a strange way, she'd become quite calm about it. Tonight The Jailer had come in, turning the lights on, flooding the room with bright whiteness and making her whole body tense in readiness. The light seemed to penetrate her entire body like an X-ray, turning it cold. She could almost imagine that she was already dead.

She listened to every sound he made, but heard nothing to suggest he was preparing for an operation. Then he'd started whistling. It was one of the classical songs he liked to play when operating and its sound gripped her heart. He was happy, a marked contrast to yesterday, but that had no bearing on whether she would live or die.

She knew it was evening because he gave them fresh water and a shake drink. Just two to prepare now. It didn't take him long.

'Early night tonight,' he'd called out to them before plunging them back into darkness.

She'd sipped at the water, but not drunk the shake. She felt no hunger, only the need to keep her throat from becoming dry.

'Sally,' she'd called out. 'Are you OK?'

She heard a faint murmur from next door.

Yesterday, as The Jailer had taken Nicky from her cell, she'd started to plead with him, begging for her life. It had been too much for Sally. She'd started to scream hysterically and bash at the door and walls of her cage as though she'd lost her mind. He'd told her to stop. Threatened to take her in place of Nicky, but she wouldn't stop screaming over and over again. Eventually, he'd taken a syringe and gone to her cell. After that, Sally had been quiet.

Her body felt numb and her own mind was struggling. There were no shreds of hope left to cling on to and she felt herself falling. She didn't even have any idea if there were people out there who would be able to help them. For weeks, months even, she'd plotted how she would overpower him and escape, but in reality, each time she stood up, she realised just how weak she was. Starvation and the complete lack of exercise had wasted away her muscles. She was feeble. She had no chance.

Her only consolation was that it would soon be over. The months of torture were behind her. She would be anaesthetised and then it would be done. She'd become a mermaid and be allowed to sleep for ever.

29

Harrison was sorely tempted to go back to Melrose House and stalk Gary Lewis. The arrogance of the man meant Harrison was worried that he'd think himself so untouchable that he'd kill again that evening just to spite them. But Harrison's practical mind kept him in his hotel room. There were two reasons. First, Gary was exhausted and, as an intelligent man, he knew it might mean he'd risk making a mistake. Second, with the weather like it was, there was no way he'd be venturing out tonight. In his twisted mind, everything had to be perfect and gale force winds wouldn't allow that.

Harrison also had a strong suspicion that he'd be sitting there smugly toasting his own triumph: the fact he'd just outsmarted them over the DNA test. It was while Harrison was imagining the chief inspector's reaction when he heard the news that Gary wasn't a DNA match, that the thought came to him. Something the chief had said during their meeting. He emailed Dr Chaudhry immediately and marked it *Urgent*.

The next morning, he could tell Tracey was nervous. Her career was on the line for this and she didn't sit still for more than five minutes, constantly checking her phone and coming back to her computer in case she'd missed something. DSU Graeme Walker had been visibly hanging around in the incident room too and there was a tension within the whole team. All of them were still working, following up other lines of inquiry and trying to identify the other two victims, but there was almost a vibration in the room, a frisson of anticipation.

While they waited, Harrison dealt with a few queries from officers back home. He received one particular email that made him smile. DI Richard Carrington had sent him a Met communications press release announcing that Finchley detectives had arrested one of Interpol's most-wanted men, Samuel Alonzo, known as Caspar the thief. Apparently he had tried to re-enter a crime scene where he was a suspect in a murder, but DI Carrington had the house under heavy surveillance, and they were able to make the arrest. Interpol said he had been responsible for the theft of millions of euros in stolen relics from churches. Needless to say, Richard was saying thank you to Harrison.

Tracey had almost worn down the carpet with all her pacing around, and she barely spoke to anyone other than to answer questions or give out orders. There was no sign of her usual jovial self today.

'Are you OK? Do you want a coffee?' Harrison asked her. He felt responsible for the current stress in her life and it looked like she could do with someone to talk to.

'Yeah sure, why not. I need to get out of here before I go crazy,' she said.

They went up to the canteen and luckily found the small

seated area was empty, with just one other officer in there ordering a toasted sandwich. Harrison remembered his first day with Tracey when he'd done the same at the coffee shop on the waterfront. That seemed like weeks ago now, not just days.

'I'm sorry that I've put you in this position of stress,' he said to her.

She looked up, surprised.

'No, you haven't. This is my investigation and I've made decisions based on what evidence I've been presented with. It's just...' she tailed off and looked out the window towards the sea. 'It's just my husband was made redundant last week. Money is going to be tight for us and I was hoping that rather than being demoted, I might be considered for promotion.' She looked at him and smiled weakly. 'It will be fine, I'm sure.'

The call came in the early afternoon. Tracey snatched at the phone, but it was immediately obvious from her face what was being said. She turned pale beneath her tan and the nervous spark of energy in her eyes deadened. All the results were negative. The mood in the incident room slumped. Within minutes Tracey's telephone rang again. Detective Superintendent Graeme Walker had called her in to his office.

She didn't say a word to Harrison, just swore to herself, brushed down her suit, took a deep breath, and went straight in.

Harrison felt for her as she undertook the walk of shame through the office, with every pair of eyes on her. He knew she was prepared to take full responsibility, but it had been him who'd persuaded her that Gary Lewis was guilty.

He was straight on the phone to Dr Chaudhry.

'I've had a lot on,' the doctor answered.

'I know, I'm sorry to push, but this could be DI Quenault's career. I need to know the answer. Do you have it?'

'Hang on, let me look, I may take a couple of minutes if you want to call me back.'

'No, it's fine. I'll wait,' Harrison urged. Keen not to run the risk of the doctor being distracted by something or somebody else.

'While I've got you on the line,' Dr Chaudhry said, oblivious to the urgency, 'we also got the analysis of the Havre des Pas mermaid's stomach contents through. She'd drunk one of those diet shakes. You know the kind, they're supposed to provide you with all the nutrients you need and nothing more. Tallies with the weight loss.'

Harrison quickly Googled Gary's health website and typed diet shake into the search bar. He was greeted by a long list of options. The site visibly proclaimed that the company had a policy to donate stock that was getting close to expiry date to charities in order to prevent waste and ensure that the vulnerable in society were receiving the right nutrients and vitamins to keep them healthy. Wouldn't be too difficult to siphon off a load of nearly out-of-date diet shakes for his own use.

It seemed like forever as Harrison listened to the doctor tapping on his computer and searching through his emails.

'Here we go. Yes, yes, they've sent through the result. Definitely, clear evidence.'

'Irrefutable?'

'Irrefutable.'

'Thank you.' Harrison ended the call while the doctor was mid flow in his response.

He jumped up, grabbing a newspaper from Tracey's desk,

and strode through the room to Walker's door, ignoring the faces that had all turned to see what he was doing. Inside, he could hear Walker's voice was strained and monotone. Harrison knocked on the door and didn't wait for an answer. He walked in.

Tracey and DS Walker looked at him in surprise.

'Dr Lane, we're in a meeting,' the detective superintendent said to him.

'I know, and I'm sorry to interrupt, but I have just received an important piece of information which I think it's critical you both know immediately.' He closed the door and moved into the room, where he could see Tracey was only just holding it together.

'I suggested yesterday, after our visit to Gary Lewis, that he had appeared too calm in the face of the DNA test. It had occurred to me that the fingernail was a little too convenient. He'd been impeccable with ensuring he didn't leave any forensic traces before now, so why would there suddenly be a fingernail, something which is excellent for getting DNA from. I asked Dr Chaudhry to run an additional test on the nail. He has just confirmed that it comes from somebody who has been taking class A drugs. The man who has been carrying out these killings could not have an addiction to drugs like that. He simply wouldn't be able to function at the level required for what we've seen.'

'OK.' The DSU was frowning as he listened. 'So that could indicate that the killer may well have planted it there to throw us off the scent, but it doesn't implicate Gary Lewis. I'm seriously concerned that this inquiry has gone down the wrong route with regard to him being its chief suspect.'

'Ah, but it does implicate him.' Harrison opened the newspaper onto Graeme's desk. 'He was with a group of men

who are either recovering or trying to recover from drug
addiction, just the day before yesterday. The day before we
found the third mermaid and the fingernail. If we were to go
and talk to the men who had been there that day, I believe we
would find the owner of the fingernail and discover that Gary
had paid him some money to supply it. They're vulnerable
individuals who would be more than happy to hand over a
nail in return for some cash.'

There was a stunned silence in the office while both DS
Walker and Tracey took in what Harrison had just said. The
superintendent read the newspaper article, his eyebrows
raised.

When Harrison looked at Tracey, she was smiling at him,
the relief evident in the rim of tears in her eyes.

'Right. Then we need to nail this bastard,' DS Walker said
to them both, leaning back in his chair, stretching his arms
behind his head – and totally missing his own joke. 'Get officers down to the drugs' rehab now and track down the fingernail donor. If we can confirm that, then maybe we might have
enough to persuade the powers that be to give us a search
warrant for Melrose House. In the meantime, how are we
going to ensure that Mr Lewis doesn't provide us with
another victim? If we pull him in to help with inquiries, he's
likely to refuse and call in his lawyers, and that might
endanger their lives further.'

'At the house, he has photographs of his daughter on
several beaches around the island – at least I'm pretty sure
they're in Jersey,' said Harrison. 'I could recognise St Ouen,
Havre des Pas and Archirondel, but maybe the others are
where he's planning on taking his other victims. If we mount
a big police presence there and let it be known publicly that
there are patrols, perhaps he will delay.'

'It's worth a try, but it won't prevent him just killing to get rid of them. If he seriously thinks we're close, he might just cut his losses and cover his tracks,' Tracey spoke now. The fire was back in her eyes.

'Then we need to keep him busy. Distract him,' said Harrison. 'I'd be happy to volunteer for that task.'

30

Harrison telephoned Gary on his mobile.

'Mr Lewis?'

'Yes.'

'Dr Harrison Lane, I was wondering if I could check something with you that's come up in our inquiry?'

'OK, fire away. I've got five minutes.'

'I mean, could I come round to your house and run something by you? It's just not going to work over the phone.'

'Look, I'm a busy man, Dr Lane. Why don't you put it in an email?'

'No, no, I'm afraid that won't work either. It needs to be in person. I'm sure you would like to be seen to be helping the inquiry?'

'I helped with the inquiry yesterday when you and DI Quenault came to my house and requested a DNA sample from me. I'm not sure everyone would have been happy to have their privacy invaded in that way.'

'Actually, it's in relation to that,' Harrison replied.

There was a few moments' silence on the other end as

Gary clearly tried to work out what Harrison could be referring to. He knew he had him. His natural inquisitiveness would mean he'd agree to the meeting.

'It will have to be quick, Dr Lane. I have a busy evening ahead of me.'

Harrison looked out the window. It was dry outside; the wind had subsided and the dark grey angry sky had been replaced by an altogether more appealing bright blue. He knew that Gary Lewis was planning on killing again tonight.

31

I t couldn't be much longer before he came in and took her to the operating table. The memory of the sounds of the saw screeched around her head. She'd not been able to get Sally to talk to her for hours. Each time she called out, there was just silence, and she feared the worst. There was no way to get to her and see if she could help. The only thing which reached her was her voice.

'Sally,' she called out again. 'What are you going to choose to eat when we get out of here? I bet Maxine, Jennifer, and Nicky have been gorging on cake and burgers since they left. I think I will have a big bowl of salted crisps and an ice-cold white wine spritzer. Soda water, not lemonade. Then I would like a crab or prawn salad, maybe both, with lots of mayonnaise. I'll follow that with steak and chips, skinny fries, and a pepper sauce. If I have room, then it has to be sticky toffee pudding and custard.

'I'll sleep in a double bed so that I can spread out like a starfish, and there will be four feather pillows on the bed so that I can have a different one for every sleep position. I'll go for a walk in the woods. Listen to the sound of the birds and the wind in the trees, and I'll wear some wellies so that I can paddle in a stream. Then I'll go home and have a hot shower. Put on my PJs and have a hot chocolate in front of a real fire and some old movie like *Gone with the Wind*, or *Casablanca*. Or maybe I'll watch *Love Actually* or *Bridget Jones*. I'll invite you all over and we'll get a takeaway and play charades and silly drinking games. It will be fun. It won't be long now, Sally, and we'll be out and free.'

32

Harrison weighed up his options. He could just go straight in there and basically hold Gary captive until Tracey came up with a search warrant, preferably by holding him by the throat. Or he could do it all legally. The face and words of DCI Sandra Barker flew into his head. She'd been a great support to him when he'd first joined the Met and started his department. *You're too valuable to be wasted on one low-life*, she'd said to him.

It wasn't the compliment so much as the practicalities behind it that resonated. He knew that if he didn't try to deal with Gary in the proper way, then it could impact on his career with the National Crime Agency and that meant he might not be able to help a victim next week, or the week after. He owed it to them to ensure that he was still able to use his knowledge to help. Tempting though the neck squeeze might be, he would do it the right way.

In which case, he decided to just go along for a chat, and see if he could keep Gary occupied long enough for Tracey to get the warrants.

. . .

HARRISON BORROWED a pool car and made his way, aided by Google Maps, to Melrose House. He buzzed at the gates and they immediately swung open to let him through. Harrison had the distinct feeling of walking into the lion's den. He'd no idea what mood he would find Gary in, but he knew he was going to have to be on his toes.

The front door was already open by the time he pulled up outside. Harrison wondered if it was a trap to get him to enter illegally and so he rang the doorbell anyway, and waited for Gary to call him in. He was sorely tempted to leave the front door slightly open in the hope that Tracey would be there soon, but he realised they would still have to get through the gates and it wouldn't take two minutes for Gary to realise that he'd left it open in this cold.

'Come on through,' Gary called to him.

He was sitting in the same room they'd been in yesterday. This time a fire was in the grate and it added a warming glow that served to highlight Gary's cold, stiff manner. He was sitting in a large, black wingback chair.

'So, Dr Lane, what is it I can do for you?'

'I'm not sure when I might have another chance to talk to you.'

'About what? The DNA test?'

'No. That was an excellent bluff, but you made a mistake, I'm afraid. Had you been less publicity hungry, then I wouldn't have known about the donation to the drugs and alcohol centre. DI Quenault is tracking down your fingernail donor right now.'

Gary smiled wryly.

Harrison continued. 'I understand the motivation. Your wife taking your daughter away must have been tough. She took complete control from you and there was nothing you could do because the courts had agreed to it. I get the mermaid theme too, but did it need to be so elaborate? Those fish tails stank. It must have been a nightmare sewing them onto the girls. Why not buy a costume tail? So much easier.'

'You wouldn't be trying to entrap me, would you Dr Lane? A convenient wire recording everything we're saying?'

'No, not at all. This is professional interest. Off the record, if you like. I've been impressed by your discipline and creativity. I may not get the opportunity to talk to you again, so I thought I'd take my chance now. It would be a shame to miss it.'

'Wouldn't it just?' Gary smiled at him. 'Well, prove to me you're not wearing a wire.'

Harrison knew this was game playing. He was trying to retain some control of the situation by being the dominant male in the room. If it meant the girls stayed alive, then he'd do it.

He took his jacket off first and turned out all the pockets, slowly. There was no rush with any of this. He needed to fill time. Then he took off his jumper and turned round, showing Gary that there was no wire visible.

'You see, no wire.'

'Oh come now, Dr Lane, you and I both know that it could be under that T-shirt of yours.' He raised one eyebrow and stared straight at him.

'No problem,' Harrison replied, smiling back and attempting to make it look genuine. He pulled his T-shirt over his head and stood facing Gary. The definition of the muscles on his bare torso was enhanced by the flickering orange flames in the fire behind him.

Gary took his time studying him. 'Impressive physique,

Dr Lane,' Gary looked at him lustfully. 'Not often you see a chest like yours.'

'Ah, I see,' Harrison said.

Gary laughed. 'Yes. Sexuality is a fluid beast, don't you think? If something is beautiful, surely that's all that matters; it should be appreciated.'

Harrison put his T-shirt and jumper back on calmly, to show that he wasn't unnerved at being the object of Gary's sexual craving, and sat down opposite him.

'So, you have some questions?'

'Well, I'm obviously going to ask you where the others are,' Harrison said, directly.

'Please don't embarrass yourself and waste my time and yours. You know I'm not going to answer that. What does it matter now? They're useless to me.'

'Are you not worried about being caught?'

'It is a consequence of the actions I took. I knew what I was doing. I'm an intelligent man, not some imbecile who thinks he can get away with anything scot-free. I'm quite looking forward to the change. My life had become dull. My little project kept me interested in the last year, but all things must come to an end. Besides, they all signed a contract agreeing to the procedures. They wanted it. I have the paperwork to show in court.'

'I don't think any of those girls wanted what you did to them. You sold them a fantasy, groomed them. The reality was a bit different.' Harrison tried hard not to sound judgemental and rile him.

'Surely that's life, is it not?'

'So how did you discover the vault room?'

'You're fishing again. No clues, Dr Lane. I'm impressed that you know about it, but you obviously have no idea how to access it. Let's just say I discovered it purely by chance and leave it at that.'

Harrison's mobile started ringing in his pocket.

'Please excuse me.'

'Of course, it might be your colleague calling you to say that she has a search warrant, or that she's on her way to arrest me.'

It was.

'Harrison, we're on our way to Melrose House. Found the guy who'd given him the fingernail. He was in hospital after overdosing thanks to the lump of cash that Gary had given him. Where are you now?'

'I'm sitting with Mr Lewis in his drawing room. We're just having a nice chat.'

'What? I hope you're not doing anything crazy. Please don't do anything stupid. We won't be long.'

'Is she worried about you?' Gary smirked. 'Left alone with the psychopath.'

'No. I think she's more worried about you left alone with me.' It was Harrison's turn to smile.

'Touché. Well, as you know, I'm not a man prone to violent outbursts. I leave that to the less intelligent. I prefer considered manipulation and if it is necessary that people have to die, then so be it.'

'What about potentially killing an entire family with a house fire?'

Gary smiled broadly.

'You really are good, aren't you! I wanted to liven Christmas up. My wife had just left me. It was my first Christmas when we weren't all together as a family the whole time. I had visitation rights, of course, but it wasn't the same.'

A buzzer sounded in the hallway.

'That's the cavalry arriving,' Gary said. 'Just press the button on the right and it will open up the gates.'

Harrison got up and went into the hallway, pressing the button he'd been told and then opening the front door and leaving it ajar.

He half expected Gary to not be there when he got back into the room, but he was still sitting in the armchair.

'I have to say that I was impressed with how quickly you saw through that ridiculous cult theory,' he said to Harrison as he re-entered. 'As if a bunch of New Age youths would have had the skillset to achieve what I did. Wasn't impressed with you calling me the mermaid butcher, though. I suspect that was when I made my mistake and gave myself away, wasn't it?'

Harrison nodded. 'Your reaction was subtle, but it was there.'

'Never mind. Jersey's little prison isn't so bad. I shall no doubt be nicknamed the mermaid killer, and there will be documentaries and books written about me. I might even write one myself. I trust that they'll let TV crews in – I can see it being a Netflix series.'

Harrison didn't have time to answer because Tracey burst into the room with two uniformed officers hot on her heels.

'Here they are, right on cue. Good evening, DI Quenault.'

She looked at Gary and then at Harrison incredulously.

'Gary Lewis, I am arresting you on suspicion of the murder of three women; one Maxine Johnson and two other victims who we have yet to identify.'

33

'I just don't understand what possessed you to come here and just have a friendly fireside chat with a psychopathic killer!' Tracey said to Harrison.

They were standing in the hallway while two officers were guarding Gary.

'I needed to be sure that he didn't have any further opportunities to hurt the remaining girls,' Harrison replied. 'I've had hundreds of conversations with psychopaths over the years. His ego is tremendous. I knew he'd actually enjoy talking about what he'd done. But the priority now is finding those girls. He wouldn't tell me where and how to get to them, and I just hope we're not too late and he hasn't already done something.'

'We've got a dog team here,' Tracey said, motioning to an officer at the front door. 'The wine cellar must be down here.'

Harrison watched as the dog and his handler disappeared down the steps into the cellar. The dog's paws pitter-pattered down, and they heard the voice of the handler encouraging him to look. A few minutes later, they reappeared, and the officer shook his head.

'Nothing.'

'OK, search the rest of the house and we'll take another look down here,' Tracey replied. 'Roberto said it was in this cellar somewhere but they'd struggled to find it, so it's not going to be easy.'

They both descended down the stairs into a square room that had shelving for wines along two facing walls. Around half the shelves were full of bottles. Harrison went first to the end walls, the most obvious clear spaces, and felt along the base of the wall and sides. He studied the floor, trying to see if there was any area that looked more worn, and he peered behind the wine racks, checking each bottle to see if one had been handled more than another.

'I can't see anything. There's no evidence of any activity down here.' He looked at Tracey.

'Maybe this vault isn't true then, maybe he has them somewhere else.' She marched straight up the stairs to the drawing room.

'Mr Lewis, I'm sure you will appreciate that we're keen to find any further victims that you might be holding captive here. It would work in your favour in sentencing if you were to tell us where they are.'

Gary shook his head. 'To be honest, I don't think it would help me at all. I may have put something in their water just before Dr Lane arrived. I suspect that you will be too late now.'

'Search the whole house and the grounds,' Tracey said to the team as she glared at Gary. 'And call an ambulance here, so we're ready.'

Harrison went back into the hall.

'He said he'd slipped them something just before I

arrived, so they have to be here somewhere. Roberto said it was at least twenty years ago, right? So memories get corrupted. Maybe he assumed the door was in the wine cellar because that's the most obvious place, but what if it isn't? We need to focus on the ground floor of the house. It could still be here somewhere.'

'Kitchen?'

Harrison shook his head.

'No, because the housekeeper wouldn't have been so vague about it then.' Harrison walked down the corridor and started to push open doors. One was a boot room, another the downstairs toilet. At the far end, the door was locked.

'Well, he's not going to give us the key to this, is he?' she said angrily.

Harrison stepped back a few paces and ran his shoulder into the door. It gave a splintering crack and opened.

'It's his office,' Tracey said as they flicked the light switch on.

'OK, let me focus. If it's here, then something should give it away.'

Harrison walked in, scanning the walls. It looked perfect. Nothing jumped out at him as being an obvious place for a secret door, and it was also impeccably tidy, which, bearing in mind Gary's character, was no surprise.

Harrison started at the base of the right-hand wall as they walked in. He was feeling for draughts of air, or cracks where there shouldn't be any, and he was looking for unusual signs of wear. Halfway round the room, he saw it.

'There. Look at the carpet: it's been flattened in front of that bookcase, but just on the one side. That has to be the entrance,' Harrison said, springing across to it.

Tracey joined him and they both tried shelves and books in the hope that one of them was the trigger to open the door.

'The knob on that cupboard is more worn than the others,' Harrison pointed to her. 'Give that a pull or push.'

She pulled it but nothing happened, and then she tried pushing it, but nothing gave. Then she grasped it and twisted. A click sounded from behind the bookcase, and Harrison was able to pull it forward like a giant door. At their feet were steps leading into a black abyss. Tracey spotted a hanging light pulley and yanked it. All of a sudden, the black hole became a white one and a small operating theatre and solid metal cages came into view. They'd found them. Question was, were they still alive?

Tracey got on her radio and asked for immediate paramedic assistance. Then she followed Harrison down the steps and into the underground vault.

The cages were solid metal, not much bigger than two double beds put together, like small oblong ship's containers. The doors were only locked with bolts on the outside, so Harrison was able to open them without any trouble. In the first, a young woman was lying still and pale on a bunk bed. The conditions were terrible, just a bucket as a toilet, and a bowl of water for washing on a metal shelf. The bed mattress was thin, and she only had a sheet to cover herself and a hospital gown for clothes. He was relieved to see that although she'd clearly undergone the same plastic surgery operations as the others, she still had her legs. Harrison felt for a pulse.

'She's alive, but only just,' he shouted to Tracey.

They could hear footsteps descending the steps.

'Over here,' Tracey called to the medics as they arrived, wide-eyed, into the underground hellhole. 'He said he put something in their water so you'll need to take that and get it analysed.'

Harrison had already moved on to the next cage. Like the

first, he found a young woman lying on a bed motionless. He felt for her pulse. 'We've got another one in here,' he shouted to the medics.

He was about to step away from her and leave the cramped cage in order to let the paramedic in when her fingers twitched and her eyelids flickered open.

Harrison smiled at her. 'You're safe. We're going to take you to hospital. It's over.'

She smiled feebly at him and reached out for his hand. 'Am I dead?'

'No, you're not. We've arrested the man who has been holding you captive and we're going to take you to hospital. You are going to be OK.'

Harrison felt hot tears in his eyes as he looked at the desperate state of the young woman in front of him.

'What's your name?' he asked.

'Abbie,' she whispered, 'my name is Abbie.'

34

Gary had just been on his way out of the door in handcuffs, heading for a custody suite, when Harrison came out of the underground vault room. Once it was clear there were no more women in there who needed medical attention, all personnel cleared out to leave the way for the forensics team.

Harrison walked straight up to Gary, who looked totally unfazed by the activity going on around him.

'So we found your secret room,' Harrison said.

Gary shrugged.

'And two girls still alive, but only just. The conditions you were keeping them in were inhuman.'

'Come on, Dr Lane, I'm a psychopath, remember? You need to tell that to someone who gives a damn.'

Harrison felt his blood rage and muscles tense, but he needed to stay calm. He had just one more question.

'So where's the sixth?'

Gary smiled broadly at him again, impressed. 'You are clever. Such a shame our chat was cut short. Yes, the youngest sister, the sixth mermaid. I'm pleased to see you're a fan of Hans Christian Andersen too. Can't stand that sickly emotional Disney rubbish. Well, my sixth mermaid will shortly be getting on a plane in Canada.'

'Your wife or your daughter?' Harrison asked.

Gary smiled at him. 'Now that one you're going to have to keep on wondering about. Can't tell you everything now, can I?' He smirked again.

The image of the two young women, now fighting for their lives in the back of an ambulance, came into Harrison's head. Anger coursed through his muscles, tensing his biceps and arms and making his jaw tighten. He could feel the urge rising in his chest to just let rip.

Then he felt a touch on his right hand, as another was gently placed on top of his clenched fist. He let out a breath, turning to see Tracey looking at him.

'He's not worth it,' she said to him gently. 'You've won, and he knows it. Don't give him the control back.'

Harrison gave an almost imperceptible nod and let his hand relax. Then he smiled back at Gary Lewis. 'That's fine. We'll make sure to let the media know all about you. Tell them that we've arrested the mermaid butcher.'

He watched as the smile on Gary's face twisted into a cold, psychopathic snarl.

35

'Jack, it's Tanya.'

'Bloody hell, what time is it?'

'It's six-thirty. Sorry, but I got the results back.'

'Results?' Jack gave a quick glance at his sleeping wife, Marie, and slipped out of bed. 'Hang on a moment.'

'The Nunhead murder weapon.'

'Of course.' Jack waited. From the sound of Tanya's voice, he wasn't expecting good news.

'It's definitely Annette Ward's blood, so it is the knife that was used.'

'And Harrison's?'

'No. No, his fingerprints and DNA aren't on the weapon.'

'Great, so that's good news. What a relief. But why did Freda Manning send it to us? I don't understand.'

'It's not Harrison's DNA. But there's a family match.'

'Holy crap, that's what Gordon said.'

'He's back today on the first flight out of Jersey, Jack. I need to get to the airport and warn him. He's not going to like it.'

. . .

HARRISON HAD to wait for his bag to finally trundle round on the Gatwick baggage hall carousel. He was relieved to be home. The mermaid case had been an emotional drain, but he had left Jersey feeling positive. One thing he did know was that he wanted to go back there soon, only this time it would be for a holiday, and maybe Tanya would come with him.

The whole island seemed to have got behind the two surviving girls. A fund had been set up for them, there were mounds of gifts donated, and Guy Kloss had offered his services free if there was any need for remedial cosmetic surgery. They were going to be OK, at least physically. Gary Lewis, on the other hand, would be spending the rest of his days in jail. He would soon get to fully understand the true meaning of being bored.

While Harrison was waiting, he turned Airplane Mode off on his phone and discovered several missed calls from Jack. There was also a text message from Tanya.

Meeting you at airport T x

That was a nice surprise. It brought a smile to his face and made him quicken his pace as he walked through the green Nothing to Declare area of Customs.

As he passed into the arrivals greeting area, she was right there in front of him. Suddenly his eyes didn't feel so tired and heavy. He walked towards her, looking forward to taking her in his arms.

'Harrison,' she said, allowing herself to be enveloped by him.

'It's so good to see you,' he replied, looking down at her and kissing her lips. 'I've missed you.'

'Me too,' she whispered, looking into his face.

'Dr Lane?' a male voice came from the right.

Harrison turned to the source of the voice. Two men stood next to him. One had brown, wavy hair and brown eyes. It was obvious that they were police detectives.

'Yes,' he replied, but he felt Tanya's hand tighten on his arm.

'Detective Inspector Gordon Jacobsen, I'm sorry to ambush you like this, but we need to speak to you urgently regarding a murder inquiry.'

Harrison turned to Tanya. She looked as though she might burst into tears.

'Are you arresting me?' he asked Jacobsen.

'I was hoping that you would be more than happy to help us with our inquiries. I appreciate that you've just got off a plane, but we need to clear a few things up. You understand?'

Harrison looked back at Tanya.

'I'm sorry,' she said. 'It's going to be OK, but there's something you need to know. I'd rather you heard it from me than in an interview room.'

Harrison frowned and waited, looking down into her eyes.

'The Nunhead murder weapon, we've just had the results, and that's when I realised...'

'Realised what, Tanya?'

'Realised what DI Jacobsen's team also discovered when they ran your DNA through the system. There's a match. It's your father.'

A LETTER FROM THE AUTHOR

Thank you for choosing *Perfect Beauties*, I do hope you enjoyed the read, and for the many of you who have been with Harrison throughout his journey, your support is very much appreciated. Reading your reviews and hearing from you is what keeps me writing and enables Harrison to keep on having new adventures. If you want to join other readers in hearing all about my new releases and bonus content:

www.stormpublishing.co/gwyn-bennett

Perfect Beauties was inspired by the plethora of mermaid stories that can be found the world over. As a child I remember wishing that mermaids were real, although having done quite a bit of research for this book, I don't think I'd like to meet some of them! This book was also inspired by the sad truth that so many young people become obsessed by another fairy story – the idea of perfection which is touted on social media and in magazines. None of us are perfect, including Harrison, who I know would want to celebrate individuality and our human condition rather than encourage a homogenous idea of what is or isn't beautiful.

As always, I'd like to say thank you to the team at Storm Publishing for helping me get this book to you, in particular my publisher, Kathryn Taussig; editor, Natasha Hodgson; proofreader, Nicky Lovick; cover designer, Tash Webber, and all the rest of the amazing support team including Melissa Boyce-Hurd.

You can keep in touch with me by joining my readers club and receive a FREE novella telling how Harrison set up the Ritualistic Behavioural Crime unit and his first explosive case, simply visit my website at www.gwynbennett.com and sign up now. You will receive news and previews of my books as well as competitions and offers. No spam guaranteed and you can unsubscribe any time.

Please also join in the conversation with me and my publisher Storm, on our social media accounts.

Thanks again to you and happy reading
Gwyn Bennett